HER CYBORG

BOUND BY HER - BOOK 3

NELLIE C. LIND

Sense of Romance

High-level romance for romance lovers!

This book also contains the short story *Tempted Cyborg*.

Her Cyborg
Bound by Her - Book 1
Copyright © Nellie C. Lind 2016
Cover and layout: Nellie C. Lind
Editor: Chrissy Szarek
Publisher: Sense of Romance
ISBN: 978-91-983128-3-6

CHAPTER 1

"So what do you think?" Doctor Jade Silva asked while typing on the keyboard in front of her.

Phoebe turned around and watched the huge TV screen on the wall.

Apart from the TV and Jade's desk, there wasn't much in the office. The lack of plants and decorations along with the white walls gave the room a clinical look.

Phoebe had a hard time sitting still. *This* was the moment she'd waited for since she signed the papers about three weeks ago.

A 3D image of a naked man was displayed to the left on the screen. He slowly rotated with outstretched arms, allowing her to see every little detail of him. On the right side, data about him blinked by, but she couldn't stop staring. He was the most handsome man she'd ever seen, and he was all hers.

Phoebe placed a hand over her mouth, pushing back a giggle. "He's perfect." She rose from the chair and walked closer to the screen.

She wanted to touch it, but that would give the wrong impression. Instead, Phoebe stared at the man, enjoyed the view of his muscular body and enchanting face.

The long, black hair lingered down his shoulders. His almond-shaped eyes looked at her. A gentle smile played on his kissable lips.

The only thing she couldn't affect was the color of his eyes, but they were the most gorgeous eyes she'd ever seen. They reminded of glass with their transparent color, and the way they shone, like cat eyes in the dark, sent goosebumps all over her skin.

About a year ago, she'd turned to the scientific and medical company MedAct to apply for a male cyborg. Relationships had never worked for her. It'd left her with a broken heart and more loneliness than she could handle, but with this cyborg, she'd never be alone again.

Phoebe had chosen his features and personality with the help of Doctor Jade Silva. She'd taken her time to decide everything, just to make sure he'd be the perfect man for her, and he was.

She was already in love with him.

The fantasy man inside her head was becoming a reality, and soon, he'd walk and breathe.

"Now, there are a few more papers to fill out," Jade said. "But once they're done, we can start the creating process. It'll take about three months before he's completed." The doctor looked up from her computer. "Do you wish to change any details? Maybe another hair color or perhaps take away an inch of his height?"

Phoebe turned to Jade. "No, I'm happy with everything."

"Are you sure? Once you press that button, it will be final, there will be no turning back."

She smiled. "I'm sure."

"Go ahead then."

Phoebe turned back to the huge TV screen and stared at the green digital button below her cyborg's spinning image.

Her hand trembled when she reached out, but she never hesitated. It clicked when she pushed it, confirming him for creation.

Chapter 2

Three months later

"Maybe I should also apply for a cyborg," Phoebe heard Faye laugh on the other side of the phone line. "I want a month away from work, too."

She laughed back. "Well, it's a little like having a baby, you know. The basic programming is already there, like eating, walking, and so on. I'll have to teach him everything else, though." A shiver of excitement went through her.

"That sounds like a lot of fun."

"So why don't you give it a try? You already have the necessary requirements. You're thirty years old, single, healthy, you have a well-paying job, and a place of your own."

"Yeah, and then there's all that testing to find out how whacked up my head is. You spent months going through that."

"It's for the cyborg's safety. MedAct wants to make sure they're with good people. You can never abandon your cyborg because of the bond. It would kill him," Phoebe said.

"And that's why I'm not sure I want to apply for one. I

like my privacy."

"You know you can give him a personality that fits you."

Faye sighed. "I don't know, Phebs. He'll be an aware being, a person of his own, like you and me, and he'll have the option to ignore his programming."

"It's your choice, Faye."

"I must admit I'm tempted, but I'll wait and see how things turn out for you before I make my decision."

"All right. I'll call you in a few days and tell you how things are going. I'm entering MedAct in a second."

"Good luck!"

"Thanks." Phoebe smiled and ended the call.

She stopped outside the huge building with more glass windows than she could count. She had no idea how many floors there were, but it seemed to be more than fifty.

Phoebe had taken her classes here and had been tested here to see if she was suitable to own a cyborg or not. Now, doctor Jade Silva and her team would have a watchful eye on both of them during the month they'd be there.

She entered through the wide glass doors. A clean and bright hall with windows instead of walls greeted her. A sign above the reception desk said "MedAct".

Today was the big day.

Today, he'd open his eyes and look at her for the first time. Nothing could go wrong.

Phoebe hurried to the elevators, dragging her wheeled bag behind her, feeling like a child who was about to open the best present ever.

People smiled when they saw her happiness.

She smiled back and stepped into the elevator. It felt like hours for it to reach the right floor.

When the doors opened on the tenth floor, Doctor Jade Silva already waited for her. Her dark brown hair was in a ponytail and she wore a doctor's coat over her black shirt and jeans.

She was a slim and short woman with a five feet, two inch frame. Her golden skin had a healthy glow that almost made Phoebe jealous. The doctor's features were sweet and gentle, but her eyes shone with strength and determination.

"Hello, Phoebe." Jade shook her hand. "Are you ready?"

"Oh, yes!" Phoebe almost yelled.

The doctor's lips twitched. "Good. Let me show you where you're staying during your visit."

Phoebe followed Jade through a long hallway. The walls were white and decorated with beautiful scone lamps. A gray carpet lay on the floor. There were white doors on both sides of the corridor, and Jade stopped in front of one of them.

She pressed a key-disk against a metallic plate next to the door. It clicked and the door opened.

They went inside.

The apartment wasn't large. There was a kitchenette, a bedroom, a small living room, and a bathroom. Everything was clinical and white. No paintings on the walls and no patterns on the curtains.

"This will be your apartment for a few weeks. Make sure

he stays in here for at least two or three days before you show him around. Remember, he won't be able to talk in the beginning. It'll take a few hours for his brain to function properly. Primitive instincts will drive him during that time, and you'll need to be there for him. Everything will be confusing."

"I understand," Phoebe said, placing her bag next to the bed.

Jade looked through the few papers that she held in her hands. "I see you have taken the shot to prevent pregnancy. That's good. You need to focus on him in the beginning while he learns. Becoming pregnant during that time is not recommended."

"I know," Phoebe answered.

She didn't want that either, but it was a dream for the future. She'd put it into his programming, but that was as far as she could go.

He had his basic programming, but he wasn't a machine. He was a constructed humanoid with cybernetic implants, created in a laboratory.

Once he opened his eyes, he'd be a person of his own, a sentient being, capable of questioning his programming.

The only thing that would never change was their bond. Without her, he wouldn't survive.

The bond was love, literally.

During her classes, the teachers taught her and the other students the importance of the bond. It was the only thing that kept the cyborgs sane. Without it, they went crazy, but most died. She didn't know why, but that was the last thing she wanted to happen to her cyborg.

"Have you chosen a name for him yet?"

Phoebe nodded. "Shade."

"That's a good name." Jade wrote it down in her papers.

Cyborgs weren't allowed to have human names like William, David, or Luke. It was a way of separating them from the humans. Instead, cyborgs had made-up names or names of things.

Phoebe didn't like that rule, but she had no choice but to follow it.

Jade lowered her papers and looked at Phoebe. "So, are you ready to meet him?"

Her heart raced. "Yes."

CHAPTER 3

Apart from the bed and the machine, the white room was empty. The lights were dim and there was a one-way window, but Phoebe didn't pay much attention to any of it. Instead, she stared at the man who lay on the bed.

His eyes were closed. Two metallic-looking cords were attached to his forehead. A machine was behind the bed, making weird, but quiet sounds. The cords other ends were attached to the machine.

Phoebe almost forgot to breathe. He was bigger than she'd imagined. His six feet four frame, broad shoulders, and muscular body was exactly what she'd wanted, and here he was.

High cheeks bones, strong jawline, full lips, and well-shaped brows adorned his handsome and masculine face. His dark and long hair lay beautifully around his head. He was like that piece of eye-candy she just couldn't get enough of.

Shade.

The name fit well to his dark features.

Phoebe couldn't wait to see his eyes. They'd be quite

something. She remembered their shiny appearance from three months ago when she'd confirmed him for creation.

Phoebe stopped in front of the bed. Her hand trembled when she placed it on his arm. The first touch sent a wave of heat through her and made her gasp.

His tan skin was warm and soft. His chest rose and sank with every breath he took.

"He'll remain asleep until we turn off the machine." Jade stood on the other side of the bed. "It will take a few seconds for his brain to activate. After that, it should take only a few moments for him to open his eyes. You need to be the first person he sees. Any confusion, and he'll easily panic. He'll look for you, and without you, pain will be the first emotion he'll experience."

"I'm not going anywhere." Phoebe couldn't look away from him.

"All right then. I'll turn off the machine now." The doctor removed the cords and pushed back the machine before pulling out a small flashlight from her pocket. She opened his right eye with her fingers and flashed him. "His brain is responding." She backed away. "Remember, he has no social skills whatsoever. He'll behave in ways you won't expect him to. He won't understand much of what you're saying either, not for the first few hours. It will be all about emotions and needs in the beginning. I'll be in the room next door, watching you both through the one-way window to make sure everything goes as planned. The hallway from this room to yours is secured. You won't meet anyone, not during the first few days while he adjusts. Seeing another human will not be good for him during that time. I'll come by to check on you both once I see it's all right to do so, but don't worry. Security cameras are all over the place. If something goes wrong, our cyborg soldiers will be by your side within seconds."

Phoebe nodded and swallowed. This was supposed to be the best day of her life. Nothing could go wrong.

Shade moved on the bed.

Phoebe almost jumped out of her skin. A gasp left her mouth.

"Good luck." Jade smiled and left the room.

Every move he made threatened to give Phoebe one hell of a shock. She clenched her hands and held her breath. All she could do was stare.

Shade tilted his head, opened and closed his mouth over and over again. A frown appeared on his forehead.

Was he trying to figure out what his mouth was?

Was his programming *this* basic?

He raised his arm but stilled when the weight of her hand stopped him. The frown deepened and he remained still for a long moment.

It was as if time itself stopped.

Then, he opened his eyes and looked at her.

Phoebe tried to remain calm, but the joy that came over her almost made her burst into tears. She barely managed to blink them away as she squeezed his hand.

Shade relaxed. Bliss filled his eyes, and it did funny

things to her core.

He looked at her with his glowing, glass-like eyes like no man had ever looked at her before. There was so much love in his gaze and no traces of doubt.

He knew who she was. It was written all over his face.

His focus was completely on her. The room didn't matter. The world didn't matter.

Only she mattered.

Phoebe placed her other hand against his cheek. A tear managed to escape and run down her own cheek.

Without ever looking away, Shade sat up. He removed the blanket and revealed a pair of white underpants, and nothing more. He exposed his body to her without a second thought.

Heat rushed to her face from the view.

Rippled muscles decorated his torso and she saw them work under his smooth and perfect skin. He made her knees week, but she managed to remain on her feet. The last thing she needed was the people behind the one-way window seeing her reaction, but they were probably used to it.

Shade sat at the bedside with his feet on the floor and pulled her closer, making her stand between his legs. His arms wrapped around her waist and his body heat linger on her skin.

Phoebe swallowed and desire awakened between her legs. Being this close to him was like a dream come true.

He studied her with his marvelous eyes and wore a gentle smile on his handsome face.

Shade made her burn like she'd never burned before in a man's presence, and that didn't surprise her. He was the man of her dreams, after all.

She'd created the perfect man for herself.

"Hi," she said softly.

His gaze dropped to her mouth and he blinked. He carefully touched her bottom lip with one finger as he raised an eyebrow.

Her pulse increased. "My name's Phoebe. Do you understand me?"

He only gave her a smile and looked at her lips again, but when she remained quiet, his gaze lowered.

Shade's hands roamed her body. First her arms, then her shoulders before he moved on to her hair. He felt it between his fingers for a few seconds. He released it and placed his face against her throat.

Her body tensed. She heard him take a deep breath as he touched her naked skin with his nose. Was he smelling her?

Cyborgs had a heightened sense of smell. All their senses were stronger than a human's, but she'd never expected him to do this. But then again, this was probably not going to be the first time he did something that would surprise her. He was a newborn cyborg and had a lot to learn.

Her heart started to pound when he pulled her even closer. Shade was strong, and his firm grip awakened a pinch of fear within her. She wouldn't be able to escape if something was wrong. The cyborg soldiers would never reach her in time. A few seconds was long enough for him to break her neck.

He pulled away and looked deep into Phoebe's eyes. His expression was serious, almost as if he was trying to read her, to understand her. His gaze returned a few times to her throat before he locked it with hers again.

Did he understand his action had scared her?

He blinked a few times and went for her arms again.

His gentle caress made Phoebe moan and her tension eased as he softly explored her. It felt so good to be touched, and she longed for more, but she had to be patient.

Right now, he was like a child discovering the world, but there was nothing coy about him. He seemed to be curious about everything.

Once he finished studying her arms, his gaze locked onto her breasts. His eyes widened, and his jaw dropped.

Phoebe knew where this was heading and the people behind the one-way window were *not* allowed to see that. She grabbed his hand. "Come with me."

His gaze jerked up to hers. Confusion filled his eyes when she backed away. He reached for her to pull her against him again, but Phoebe grabbed his other hand and tried to get him to stand.

"It's all right." She smiled.

Even if he didn't understand her words, she hoped he understood the calm and gentle tone in her voice. She encouraged him to follow, and eventually, he rose from the bed.

She led him toward the door and opened it into the hallway.

Shade followed without a doubt. His gaze never left her.

CHAPTER 4

Everything felt strange, as if he'd been asleep for a long time. His mind was fuzzy, he couldn't think straight, and yet, he somehow knew he'd just awakened.

Many thoughts came and went, but he was unable to catch them. When he had one in his grasp, it disappeared somewhere in the distance, fogging his mind again.

But he didn't care, none of that mattered. What mattered was the beautiful redheaded woman in front of him. She had a tall and slender figure. She seemed strong, and yet, delicate. Her facial features were perfect with big, green eyes, straight nose, and plump lips.

There was no other woman, and never would be.

Nothing would take him away from her. He would protect her with his life.

Instinct told him he belonged to her. Everything about her appealed to him. Touching her wasn't enough anymore, though. He needed more now. A lot more. He couldn't satisfy his hunger for her. The ache between his legs grew along with his desire. He needed to ease it and only she could make it happen.

She was leading him somewhere, but he wasn't interested in where. Instead, he wanted to touch her, feel her, and worship her body.

His woman said something and smiled. It was a smile to die for, but her words didn't make sense. It was almost as if he knew their meaning, he just couldn't place them, but the sound of her voice was like the gentlest touch.

He couldn't keep his hands to himself, but her walking made it difficult to touch her. He wanted her to stand still. The ache in his body kept growing, and a feeling of despair filled him.

If only she could stop for just one minute!

He grabbed her arm and pushed her gently against the wall.

Surprise crossed her eyes and he realized he needed to be careful. He'd managed to scare her once already. He never wanted to do that again. She was as new to him as he was new to everything.

He pressed himself against her and laced her arms around his shoulders. Her body heat and nearness fed his starving desire. He grabbed one of her legs and placed it around his waist, bending down a little and pressing his aching need against her core.

A moan escaped their mouths and she closed her eyes. He smiled. She liked this. He did it again and tried to show her that he needed her to touch him, but she didn't comply. Instead, she giggled, and her cheeks turned red.

He stilled and looked at her face. She looked so cute

with the blush on her cheeks.

She shook her head, and gently pushed him away, making him let go of her. She said something again. He still had no idea what, but he knew what the shaking meant. She wasn't going to let him touch her. She couldn't be serious! Didn't she see how much he needed her? He'd burst from need soon.

He'd never go against her wishes, but he was incapable of listening right now. His need was painful and all he wanted was to strip her naked right here and right now.

She looked down the hallway and pointed as she continued talking. She tried to pull him in that direction, but he didn't want to go. There was nothing down there that wasn't right here.

He silenced her by pressing his lips against hers. For a split-second, she tensed but it didn't take long until she eased into his kiss. He opened her mouth with his and pressed his tongue against hers.

Happiness sang inside him when she didn't stop him. Maybe she understood his desperate need. He had no idea why it was so intense, but he knew she had to take care of him, and she had to do it *now*.

His heart pounded. He panted and sweat broke out on his skin. His body even trembled, and the feeling became more uncomfortable by the second.

She said something again between his kisses, and this time, he managed to understand one word. She'd said "room".

He stilled and looked down the hallway as she pointed again.

Room.

Yes, he knew what a room was, but why did she want to go there? This place was just as good. There was no reason for them to go to a room.

He leaned into her again and showered her throat with kisses. She moaned and it filled him with pride. He was making her feel good. The way she rubbed herself against him told him so, too.

"Camera," she panted.

He met her gaze when he realized he'd understood another of her words. A second word that hadn't sounded like a pointless sound.

Camera? What the heck was that? And why did it matter? Couldn't he just finish this?

She turned her head to the side and looked up.

He followed her gaze and noticed something not too big, metallic, and black hanging down from the ceiling.

Camera.

Images and information streamed into his mind from the second he laid eyes on that strange black thing. For a short while, he stood frozen while staring at it. Within seconds, he went from not having a clue what that little box was, to knowing everything about it.

Camera.

Yes, it was filming them, and someone was able to see everything they did. The red dot near the lens told him so.

He looked at her again.

Room.

Camera.

Yes, he understood.

She wanted to get away from the camera. She wanted to go to a room somewhere down the hall.

He made a decision. In an instant, he lifted her up and ran down the hallway.

She let out a squeak and laughed.

CHAPTER 5

The moment Phoebe told him to stop in front of their temporary apartment, Shade put her down and lunged at her. Getting the key card out from her pocket wasn't the easiest when Shade's arms started exploring her.

His arms moved around her body while he pressed his lips against her throat, kissing, and licking her sensitive skin.

The sensation made her moan and almost drop the key card, but somehow, she managed to open the door the second before he stripped her of the t-shirt.

Phoebe closed the door behind them and he threw the t-shirt to the floor before he reached for her again. She'd been told the first hours of his life would be all about needs and emotions, but she hadn't expected this.

His eyes were big, he breathed fast, and he was in a hurry. He didn't let her move toward the bed. Instead, he pressed himself against her as if he couldn't get her close enough. His desire shone right through him. His desperation was just as clear. He'd wanted to take her in the hallway, but somehow, she'd managed to get him into the room.

Maybe he'd understood what she'd said. It had seemed

like it, and it'd made her happy. His understanding of words was awakening faster than she'd expected.

Something told her this would be fast and hard, maybe even against the wall instead of the cozy bed she'd looked forward to, but she didn't mind. Instead, she smiled and kissed him back when his lips pressed against hers. The feeling of his tongue against hers sent waves of pleasure through her.

Barely a minute later, he had her naked. His underpants went next. He kicked the clothes away with his foot without ever taking his hands or lips off her.

His warm breath against her skin felt amazing. This was what she'd longed and dreamed of for so long, to finally be in the arms of her imaginary lover. She caressed his back, enjoying the feeling of his soft skin under her fingers.

Shade's hand landed on her breast. He squeezed it before his fingers found her nipple and rolled it between his fingertips.

Phoebe arched her back as the sharp pleasure from his touch went right through her. It made her head spin and her body tremble.

He grabbed her bottom with both hands, and with one swift move, he lifted her up, making her wrap her legs around him as he pressed her back against the wall.

Excitement rose within her. She'd been ready for him ever since he'd opened his eyes.

He moved closer, first feeling with his shaft, making sure he wouldn't hurt her, and when he found the right place, he thrust forward, determined, but gentle.

Phoebe gasped when he entered her. Another wave of pleasure hit, filling her from the inside out.

Shade tossed his head back. A deep and masculine groan left his throat. His hips started to move, slowly at first, then faster.

Each stroke made her forget the world around them. There was only them. She felt safe in his arms, but there was also no escaping. He was strong and determined. He knew what he wanted, and all Phoebe could do was lean her head against his shoulder, close her eyes, and *feel*.

He lacked restrictions. He was wild, loud, and if anyone interrupted him, Phoebe knew they'd regret it for the rest of their lives, but at the same time, no one was that stupid. A newborn cyborg wasn't to play around with when it came to bonding with its bound one.

Phoebe had never heard of a failed bonding, but everyone knew what would happen if one did fail. The doctors were clear on the matter.

Never leave your cyborg, don't let him experience fear, doubt, or pain during the first crucial days of his life because those feelings would later drive him.

A dangerous cyborg was more dangerous than a human could ever be. They were stronger than humans, capable of developing an intellectual mind beyond human capability, and they never forgot - anything.

Once the bond was made, the cyborg would never want to leave its bound one. Why would they when their love for their bound one surpassed everything? They would die to defend their bound one.

Shade bonded himself to her at this very moment. His groans, his solid grip, his desire, and the ecstasy written all over his face told her so.

Phoebe loved it, but not only that, she loved him. She always had, even when he'd been just a fantasy.

The difference was that he was finally real, and his touch was like no one else's. This was her place, in his arms, to love him, to care, and to cherish him. She always would.

Shade tightened his hold and his thrusts became even more determined. He was close and so was she.

A few more strokes was all it took before her body ignited. She felt herself tighten around him as her orgasm rocked through her body, and that was it for him. His moans turned into a roar as he came.

His body shook and the feeling of him tensing inside her as he filled her with his release made her smile and love every second of it.

Silence and hard breathing followed.

Phoebe felt the perspiration and the heat from his skin against hers. He was warm all over, but so was she.

Slowly, he lowered her legs and she couldn't help but wonder if an awkward moment would come next. At first, she barely dared to look him in the eyes. She expected to see confusion, but instead, she was met by a sated smile.

She placed her hand against his cheek and the happiness her touch seemed to bring him went straight to her heart, making her look forward to the month they'd spend here.

They'd have so much fun together. She'd make sure of it. She'd teach him everything he needed to know during the day, and during the night, they'd hold each other tight, maybe during the day as well. She doubted they'd be able to keep their hands away from each other.

His slowly rising shaft told her so.

She grabbed his hand and led him to the bedroom. "Come."

He didn't protest.

Shade had no clue what a computer or a car was, not even what a book or a flower was, but that would soon change.

Within a few hours, he'd be able to talk and understand the world around him, but for now, she was his whole world. He still hadn't looked away from her even once to examine his environment. Right now, he needed to feel loved and happy, and she intended to give him that.

All night long.

CHAPTER 6

Phoebe yawned and opened her eyes. She lay on the bed in her temporary apartment with no clothes on. Her gaze turned to the clock that hung on the wall, it was almost noon. She'd been asleep for about seven hours.

That wasn't very long, considering how exhausted she'd been after the wild night with Shade. He'd worn her out completely. He hadn't let her go for five seconds. He'd been her shadow.

She couldn't remember how many times they'd made love, but her sore body whispered of many times. Her lower parts still hadn't recovered, but the discomfort didn't bother her. It was a gentle reminder of Shade's embrace.

He had been amazing, loving, and caring. Strong, determined, and raw. Gentle, sweet, and cute. He'd even been happy, and they'd laughed together, even if he hadn't been able to understand much of what she'd said. His pleased expressions after every orgasm had been a pleasure to watch, but eventually, she'd slipped away to the world of dreams.

Phoebe turned on the bed and froze.

It was empty.

Her heart started to race. This wasn't good. "Shade?"

No answer.

Phoebe rose from the bed and covered herself with the blanket.

She hurried to the living room and relaxed when she spotted him standing by the window.

He didn't have a single piece of clothing on and he stood with his back toward her.

Her gaze lowered to his muscular behind and she swallowed. The sight of him spread sweet heat through her as she remembered what they'd done just a few hours ago. And now, she couldn't help but stare at the fit and muscular body she'd given him with the help of Jade and her team of doctors.

"Shade?"

He didn't turn around. Didn't move.

Phoebe hoped nothing was wrong, that he hadn't malfunctioned. Seven hours was a long time for a newborn cyborg to be on his own. Who knew what he'd done during her sleep.

His development would happen fast now and wouldn't slow for a couple of days. She should've been there for him. She should've forced herself to remain awake.

She approached him, not really sure of what to do.

"You woke me up," he said with a dark and deep voice.

Phoebe froze just two steps away and stared at his back.

He'd spoken and without difficulties.

"Yes," she answered.

"Why am I here?"

She gulped. What did you answer to a question like that? "Because I love you," she said after a short silence.

Shade turned and looked at her with his marvelous glass-like eyes. "I love you, too. I belong to you. I feel it in here." He pressed his hand against his chest.

Phoebe nodded, but his emotionless expression made her tense. Didn't he like being in love with her and belonging to her? She hadn't really given him a choice in the matter, but at the same time, things couldn't be any other way.

A cyborg had to have a powerful bond. That was the law and there was nothing more powerful than love. A cyborg who lost his bound one rarely survived the loss, but those who did survive became shadows of their former selves, and most went crazy. So, it was either a bond or death for them.

The loss of the bond made them dangerous, unpredictable, and unstable. Those who refused to bond themselves to a new bound one joined the Fighters, a group of ownerless cyborgs that lingered somewhere outside of town.

"Does it bother you?" she asked.

"No. There's nothing more I want than to be with you. I will always protect you, stay by your side, and give up my life to defend yours."

Her heart raced. His devotion was clear and she pushed aside the thought that his love for her was forced upon him.

Would he have fallen in love with her if he'd been a human?

She needed the answer to be yes. It was yes. It had to be, and not make it more complicated than that. She'd been through these types of thoughts during the first few months of her evaluation to find out if she was suitable to be the bound one of a cyborg or not.

Phoebe had listened to the teachers at MedAct and learned everything there was to learn about the cyborgs. She'd gone through many tests, especially mental tests, and once approved, she'd received her diploma. It'd been the happiest day of her life, and now, she was happier than ever before.

He was here now, just a step away from her, evaluating his surroundings. But at the same time, she couldn't help but wonder if he was fine with *everything*.

She'd been taught that cyborgs didn't question their own existence and their bound one's reasons for creating them. They just went along with it. As long as they were happy, and their bound ones cared about them and loved them, there was nothing they *needed* to question.

Phoebe had met a few cyborgs during her time in school, cyborgs that belonged to the teachers or doctors who worked for MedAct. None of them had looked unpleased with their fate. Instead, the love for their owners had been obvious.

Cyborgs weren't common, though. They were expensive and not everyone could afford one.

She was grateful that the company she ran from home gave her enough money to fulfill that dream. She ran a marketing company and she was one of the best out there.

People didn't seem to mind paying extra for her services because once she was in the picture, everything came alive.

"You must have questions," she said.

"Yes, and I will ask them at the right time." His voice was determined, and his straight posture said he knew what he wanted, how he wanted it, and when he wanted it, and no one could tell him otherwise.

It was a characteristic she'd chosen for him. She'd wanted a strong cyborg who wouldn't be afraid to stand up for her, and she saw just that in his eyes. With Shade by her side, she'd always be safe.

He moved closer.

Phoebe held her breath. She couldn't stop ogling him. His front was impressive with the six-pack abdomen and hairless chest. Heat rushed to her cheeks.

"It pleases me that my body appeals to you," Shade said. "I'll make sure you're always thoroughly satisfied."

She gave him a shy smile and expected him to joke away his words. She was so not used to hearing a man talking like that, but his face remained serious. Phoebe gasped when he grabbed the blanket and tried to pull it away from her. "What are you doing?"

"Your body temperature is rising. You need satisfaction."

He was right about that, but her lower parts didn't agree. She was still sore.

"Let go of the blanket," he demanded. "Your satisfaction cannot be achieved when it's in the way."

"I know, but I think we should talk before we ... you know."

Shade released the blanket. "As you wish."

Phoebe blinked.

She'd expected him to disagree and take the blanket anyway, but he'd obeyed instead.

It hit her. He'd never go against her decisions.

She had the final say in everything, whether he liked it or not, at least as long as he was a newborn cyborg.

What awaited in the future, she couldn't tell, but the future didn't matter. What did matter was getting him onto his feet, showing him the world, and teaching him everything he needed to know.

Phoebe watched him, and he watched her.

His expression was tense, and his fists were clenched. He breathed fast and when she looked down, she saw his strained shaft.

It hit her again.

Emotions still drove him, and they would continue to drive him a few more days. He needed her, but she'd turned him down. Despite that, he'd obeyed.

The burning desire in his eyes and the way Shade licked his lips as he ogled her made his desire impossible to miss.

Phoebe couldn't allow him to suffer.

Surprise darted across his face when she kneeled in front of him. He opened his mouth, maybe to ask her what she was doing, but he went silent when she grabbed his shaft and licked the tip.

He gasped and Phoebe smiled.

This was going to be good.

CHAPTER 7

Shade lay on the bed and stared at the ceiling. He was exhausted but satisfied. He'd just come down from another exquisite height Phoebe had taken him to.

Her sweet and gentle hands had explored him in the most teasing and enjoyable ways. They'd barely done anything but touch each other these last two days.

Few words had been exchanged, but it didn't matter. He was happy, and so was she. He saw it on her smile and he felt it in her caresses. As long as he could make her smile, he was doing the right thing.

The world around him had become clearer. He was still somewhat confused, even if he understood more. The fog in his mind wasn't that much of a problem anymore. It was slowly going away.

Shade could focus now, and when he looked around the room, he knew by instinct what most of the things were. He knew that he lay on a bed, that the blankets were white, and what every part of his body was called.

Phoebe didn't have to explain everything to him. He learned by himself. It was somehow embedded deep inside his mind, and all it needed was a tiny push to awaken, but there were still a lot of things he needed to learn. She'd help him with that. They just needed to get out of the bed first.

He studied things while she lay exhausted in his arms. The technical things were easiest to understand. All he had to do to find out what they were meant for was to connect his mind to them. Within minutes, he'd learned how to use the computer, the television, and the holographic telephone.

Other things, like how to use the bathroom or the kitchen, clicked as soon as he saw Phoebe use them. Of course, he didn't follow her into the restroom, unless to shower with her, but she didn't need to explain how to use the shower or the toilet.

But the world outside the windows was still a mystery. He'd stood by the windows several times while she'd slept, just studying everything, wondering, and thinking.

He put his arms around the woman who lay on top of him. He held her tight and didn't want to let go. She didn't struggle under his firm grip. Instead, she cuddled her face against his neck.

Phoebe.

Shade had known her name from his first breath. He'd learned his name, Shade, when she'd called out to him two days ago from the bedroom. He liked it. It was her gift and he'd carry it with pride.

Somehow, he knew he was different from the woman in his arms. The difference between them wasn't big. He looked like a human, but he wasn't a human. He knew he was a cyborg. He'd known from the first moment he'd opened his eyes.

He was a humanoid, with cybernetic implants and processors. Shade was a lot stronger than a regular human, learned faster, had a photographic memory, and he wouldn't age. He healed faster and was difficult to kill compared to a human. He could fight, defend, and protect. In short words, he was the perfect killing machine, and yet, here he was, meant for loving a woman and making her happy instead of going to war.

He eased his grip on her and caressed her back with the tip of his fingers. A pleased sigh came from Phoebe and that simple sound boosted his ego. His bound one was happy.

Shade leaned closer and pressed his nose against her skin. He inhaled deeply, letting her scent fill his senses. It had a calming effect on him. He could lie like this all day long.

Phoebe.

He was hers whether he wanted it or not. He hadn't been given a choice. His programming told him he had to be bound to a human to live. His programming also told him that cyborgs without a bond to a human went crazy and he didn't want that.

Besides, he didn't mind belonging to Phoebe. She was attractive; beautiful from the inside out. He liked the way her cheeks blushed and the way she smiled when he looked deep into her eyes. He was *her* creation.

She'd created him from the bottom of her heart. She felt as bound to him as he felt bound to her. He knew that.

Shade had some details about her, information that had been put inside his mind, so he'd know from the start whom he belonged to. Phoebe had had a good upbringing with loving parents, but they'd passed away in a car accident about ten years ago. She'd been an only child and spent a lot of time with her best friend Faye growing up. Today, their relationship was tight, and they told each other everything.

Shade had no idea what Faye looked like, but he knew she had a strong and stubborn personality. It'd been added to his information bank inside his programming.

Phoebe worked from home with her marketing business, whatever that was. She'd made her fortune thanks to her company, and she was proud of it.

Even if he'd never seen money, he knew what it was, but he didn't know how to use it. Shade knew this was something he needed to learn on his own because some things only came with experience.

She lived in Glaswell, a community just outside of town. He didn't know what it looked like there, but it was an area where people with money lived. It was well protected behind a high wall, bringing people peace and safety from the outside world that wasn't always the safest place.

Shade caressed her cheek. She'd been lonely over the years. She'd been in a bad relationship that had almost destroyed her, and it'd taken her a long time to get over it.

Phoebe had been on her own ever since and had hated it. That was why she'd applied for a cyborg. She'd considered it to be her last chance for happiness, and she'd been right.

Shade would never make her cry, never make her sad and angry. He was hers to command, and he felt compelled to do what she wanted as long as it wasn't bad or wrong. He could tell her no if he wanted, if it was the right thing to do.

He wasn't a machine who'd follow his bound one blindly. It didn't work like that, and even if she'd created what she believed to be the perfect man for her, they still needed to get to know each other and make their relationship work, just like any other couple. Shade had his basic programming, but his life experience could, and *would* change him.

One thing was sure, though. He'd die for her. He'd do everything in his power to protect her from anything he considered a threat. She was his to keep safe, and if anyone tried anything, they'd pay with their blood.

The bond he felt for her was so strong it almost overwhelmed him. He didn't want to be separated from her. He'd follow her anywhere she went, whether she wanted him to or not. She was stuck with him now. *Period*.

Phoebe moved in his arms. She yawned and looked at him with sleepy eyes.

Shade turned them onto their sides, and when she lifted her leg and placed it on his hip, he knew what she wanted.

He was hard for her pretty much all the time. The intense need for her wasn't as desperate as it'd been the first day, but it was still there. He still needed her several times each day.

Shade moved a little, and without much effort, he found her entrance. She closed her eyes when he pushed inside.

A pleased moan left her mouth.

Passion took slowly over. Shade would never grow tired of this. The feeling was amazing and beyond anything else. He wanted to stay like this forever, moving slowly inside her while he held her in his arms.

Phoebe still looked sleepy, but a smile decorated her sweet features. It was a smile that reached the deepest part of him. He needed that smile to satisfy his hunger for her. An emotional hunger that would never leave him.

She placed a hand on his rear end to make him move faster. Shade obeyed. The slow pace was starting to frustrate him, too. The need to come grew and he entered her deeper as he pressed himself against her.

"Don't stop," she groaned. "I'm close ..."

Passion fogged his mind. It took over him, couldn't stop. He was beyond the point of stopping. He hung on a thin thread between complete satisfaction and frustration.

Shade closed his eyes and wrapped his arm around Phoebe, placing his face against her throat while he thrust in and out with desperation.

Phoebe moaned, and it didn't take long before she trashed underneath him. She screamed out her pleasure way too close to his ear, but Shade didn't care. When her inner muscles clamped around his shaft, he was done for.

The passion hit him in the spine, traveled fast to his balls, and filled his shaft. He exploded inside her with a roar. His body jerked, his head spun, and his toes curled.

Afterward, they lay in each other's arms in silence. Words weren't necessary. Phoebe eventually fell asleep from exhaustion.

He was a newborn cyborg after all and demanded a lot from her during his first few days. It was nothing he could control. That was just the way it was, but she didn't seem to mind, even if he had to awaken her several times each night.

About an hour later, she opened her eyes again and gave him a pleased but tired smile. "Do you need me again?"

Shade shook his head. "I can wait. You need to rest."

"The urges aren't that bad anymore?"

"No. They don't drive me like they did yesterday."

"That's good. How does your head feel?"

"Clearer with each passing hour. I understand now what most things in here are. I can also think easier."

Phoebe took a deep breath and gave out a pleased sigh. "So, it's going in the right direction. One more day, or two, and you'll be ready for the next step."

"Yes." Shade went silent for a while. "What's the next step?"

Phoebe licked her lips and didn't answer at once. "Meeting the doctor who created you."

"Doctor Jade Silva."

She nodded. "You know her name."

"I have basic information about her. She was the supervisor during my creation. She followed your wishes to the letter. I've had them all programmed into my mind. I even look just like you wanted me to."

She watched him for a while. "Are you pleased with your looks?"

He frowned. "Shouldn't I be? If it makes you happy that

41

I look like this, then I'm happy, too."

"There isn't anything you wish to change?"

Another strange question. "Why would I want that?"

She shrugged. "I don't know. I'm just trying to figure you out."

"I see." He smiled and relaxed. "I'm fine. Don't worry."

Phoebe smiled back and sat up. "How about I question you about the things you see in here?"

He grinned. It wasn't necessary, but she wanted to be reassured. The joy in her eyes told him she looked forward to it. She needed it. It would make her feel better to know he was evolving as he should.

"Why not," he said.

Her smile widened and she got up, grabbed her nightgown, and put it on. It was a cute little thing in light pink, with straps instead of sleeves. It barely reached her knees and lay perfectly around her bust.

The sight of her in it made his body react. Heat traveled to his shaft, making him hard under the linens, but he tried to control it. Phoebe needed a break.

She approached the wall and pointed at the big, dark, flat device that hung on it. "What is this?"

"It's a television. A telecommunication device used to entertain with sounds and moving images in mostly two or three dimensions. The first televisions had black and white images, but as time moved forward, color took over, and today, you can watch a television program with holographic images that make you feel as if you're right in the middle of the show."

Her chin dropped, her eyes widened, and she stared as if she couldn't believe what he'd just said. "How can you know all that?"

"My cybernetic implants give me the ability to connect myself to any technical device that isn't password protected. By doing so, I can study it from the inside out and learn everything there is to know about it."

Phoebe blinked. "I didn't know that. They never mentioned that during my studies."

He sat up. "What did you learn?"

"Well, mostly the basics, and they wanted to find out if I was fit to ... own a cyborg." She shook her head. "I don't like that saying, but that's what they call it. The tests are harsh, especially the mental ones. They need to be sure that the people who are given a cyborg are healthy and strong, and that they won't regret creating one."

He nodded. "We die without the bond."

"Yes, most of you do."

"Those who survive go crazy."

"Yes, that's what they taught me."

That was also what his programming told him.

Phoebe looked at the television again. "But how did you learn all the historical information about it? I doubt you read it in the circuits."

He grinned. "No, the Internet told me."

She blinked again. "You can use the computer when it's not turned on?"

"Yes. I can learn that way, too, but I haven't touched

43

it much. The Internet is a messed up place with a lot of confusing information. It overwhelmed me. So I decided to stay away from it for now."

"That was probably wise." She looked around the room. "I guess asking you what everything is, is kind of pointless then."

"No, it's not. I know what most of the things are, but it doesn't mean that I understand everything."

"Oh." Phoebe smiled. "So ... do you want to watch something? Maybe there's an interesting tv-show running."

Shade shook his head. "It's not necessary. I prefer talking to you. We haven't done much of that yet." He pulled off the cover and stood. His erection was still there, refusing to calm.

Her gaze lingered down his body and locked onto his shaft before she looked away and her cheeks turned pink.

Pride filled him. Hopefully, he'd always have this effect on her.

"I see you need me again," she said.

"Yes, but it can wait."

She licked her lips. "Are you sure?"

The want and the need in her eyes made him doubt his decision. Damn, he still wasn't the best at controlling his desire. He wanted her again even if he'd just had her.

Phoebe walked toward him, but instead of stopping in front of him, she stopped behind him. She placed her hands on his back and caressed him.

He closed his eyes. Her touch was gentle and soothing.

It felt like heaven. Her hands moved around on his body, making him enjoy every second. Shade needed this, all the time. It didn't matter how much they cuddled, kissed, or made love. He didn't stay satisfied for long.

He tensed when she pressed her cheek against his back while her hand traveled toward his shaft. Shade moaned when she grabbed him firmly. Slowly, she moved her hand up and down, paying plenty of attention to his tip, making him shiver all over.

"So what do you want to talk about?" Phoebe asked.

"Talk?" He could barely focus on anything but her sweet fingers.

She giggled. "Yes. You said you wanted to talk."

Shade groaned. "Make me come first, then we'll talk."

She rubbed him faster. "But what if I want to talk now?"

His muscles tensed when her other hand landed on his behind. She pinched him.

He gasped and the need to come grew. Phoebe was teasing him, and for a second, he feared she'd stop. He was unable to answer her the closer he came to reaching his peak, but hopefully, she wasn't expecting an answer.

The tension in his body grew, and when Shade could no longer hold back, the amazing feeling grabbed him. It gathered in his shaft while her grip tightened and she worked him with determination.

He came with a loud roar as she emptied him of everything he had. Perspiration broke out on his skin. His knees wobbled, barely holding him up as his heart pounded.

A short silence followed before she let go of him. She approached the bed and reached for the towel that lay beside it. Phoebe dried her hands and handed him the towel.

His mind was still foggy from the exquisite height she'd taken him to. His knees wanted to give in, but somehow, he managed to remain on his feet. He dried himself and sat down on the bed, blowing out a breath.

"Feeling better?" she asked with a grin.

"Yes," he answered.

"Good. Now, we can talk."

Shade remained sitting while pulling himself together. His legs were still shaky, but eventually, he was able to stand again. He put on underwear and pants.

"Anything special you wish to talk about?" Phoebe asked.

He approached the window and looked out. Wherever he looked, there were tall buildings with glass-like exteriors. There were cars, and buses flying around or driving on the roads below. People walked, heading in different directions. There was a park not far from the building they were in.

The sun shone high in the sky and it was a beautiful day, but for him, it looked chaotic. So many things at the same time went on. In a few days, he wouldn't have any problems handling it, but right now, when his mind still wasn't working properly, it overwhelmed him.

Phoebe stood beside him. "What are you thinking?"

"That I don't want to go out there."

"Why not?"

He bit his lower lip. "Too much."

She placed her hand on his arm. "You don't have to watch if you don't want to. Everything is still new to you, but when the time comes for us to leave, you'll be ready."

He nodded. "Yes." Shade went silent for a while. "Is it like this everywhere?"

"No. We're in the middle of a big city, and here, you can't expect anything else. Where I live, things are calmer."

"Good. I prefer that."

She smiled. "I know."

He smiled back. "Tell me more about where you live."

"It's a small town called Glaswell, not far away from here. Around three thousand people live there. There are no tall buildings there, just big villas and plenty of green fields and parks. We have a shopping mall along with other things we need, and everything is behind high walls that keep intruders out. Other cyborgs live there as well. You'll be able to meet them and they'll help you adapt."

"I'd prefer you did that."

Phoebe gave him an understanding smile. "And I will, but I don't want you to be alone while I work. I'm sure they'll want to be friends with you."

"Work." Shade frowned without ever taking his gaze away from the lively city outside the window. "Will I work?"

"If you want."

"What do the other cyborgs do?"

"Anything they want. Wind, for instance, paints. He makes amazing paintings together with his bound one, Diane, but she's sick."

"What's wrong with her?"

"All I know is that she has a heart disease, but she doesn't talk about it."

"What will happen to Wind if she dies?"

"I don't know what Diane is planning, but the only thing that can save Wind is another woman for him to bind himself to."

Shade watched her as silence filled the room.

Sadness and worry lingered in her eyes. Phoebe seemed to know Wind and Diane, but he had no files about them. She'd never mentioned them to Doctor Jade Silva, but it didn't matter. What did matter was to keep her safe, and he'd protect her from anything or anyone who tried to hurt her.

Anyone.

Chapter 8

Phoebe looked Shade in the eyes. There was a seriousness that hadn't been there before. It was almost on the verge of possessiveness and anger. She swallowed and realized her mistake. Maybe she shouldn't have told him about Wind and Diane.

He was still a newborn cyborg and even if he learned fast, he still had a lot to understand. To know that Wind would soon lose his bound one was the last thing a newborn cyborg needed to hear.

Shade took a step closer and entered her personal space.

His powerful gaze made her feel tiny and vulnerable with his tall, and muscular but, oh-so-appealing physic.

"Know this," he said with a deep voice. "You're mine to protect and I'll do everything in my power to keep you safe from anyone or anything that tries to hurt you."

Phoebe clenched her jaw. She wanted to tell him he couldn't protect her from death. It would happen one day, and he would be left alone because cyborgs lived longer than humans, a lot longer. That was, if he survived her death. She doubted the scientists had thought things through when they'd given the cyborgs a longer lifespan.

There was a knock on the door.

Phoebe startled. She turned away from Shade and headed for the front door, but before she'd taken two steps, a hand grasped her arm.

Shade looked even more serious than a minute ago. "Where are you going?"

"Someone knocked. I have to open the door."

His gaze lingered to it when a second knock came. He let her go and approached the door with determined steps.

Surprise filled Phoebe when he jerked it open and blocked the entrance with his massive frame.

Jade, who stood on the other side, winced. She stared at Shade with huge eyes, but after a short moment, she gave him a smile and relaxed. "Hello, Shade. It's nice to meet you. Do you know who I am?"

"You're Doctor Jade Silva," he said with a cold voice.

"Yes, I am. May I come in?"

"No."

"It's been two days. The worst should be over for you, and your mind should be working, but I need to check. I need to see that everything is fine with you."

"I feel fine. Now leave."

Jade didn't seem worried by Shade's threatening posture. "You know I can't do that. I'm here to check how Phoebe is doing as well. You need to let me in."

His voice darkened. "Do you really believe I'd hurt Phoebe? She has been with me for two whole days and she's still breathing."

"You're entering the second phase now, and you're going to need help."

Phoebe clenched her knuckles. In the second phase, things could go really wrong, and without help, Shade wouldn't make it through the day.

His mind had evolved fast and the basic things were now in place, like talking, eating, and understanding his body. But the second phase had everything to do with *her*. He was bound to her, and his mind had to learn to accept everything around her. Like other men, for instance.

"Fine," Shade said, "but they're not coming in."

Curiosity awakened in Phoebe. She hadn't seen anyone else but Jade. Shade's large frame hid everything from her view. She leaned to the right and noticed two male cyborgs standing near the doctor in the hallway.

And not just any cyborgs.

They were cyborg soldiers — specially designed to protect the humans from the cyborgs.

Both were massive with broad shoulders, muscles wider than her thighs, huge hands, and about seven feet tall.

Jade nodded, but instead of making room for her, Shade backed.

Surprise hit Phoebe once again when Shade stopped in front of her, grabbed her arm, and pulled her behind him.

The doctor left the door open.

The cyborg soldiers stopped in the door frame, making Shade tense and his grip on her arm tightened, but he wasn't hurting her.

The two cyborgs had short, blond hair, and they were dressed in black military clothing. They had guns and batons by their hips. They gave out a don't-mess-with-me vibe, and even if she understood that they were here for Jade's safety, Phoebe wanted them gone. She didn't doubt they'd use their weapons on Shade if they found it necessary.

"Don't worry, Phoebe," Jade said. "This is normal behavior. He doesn't understand how to handle the other cyborgs and me being near you. He's never met another human or other cyborgs before and his first instinct is to defend you. Rain and Dare won't hurt him."

Phoebe nodded, trusting Jade's words. "Are they your cyborgs?"

"No, I don't have a cyborg. They belong to other scientists who work for MedAct."

"Oh." Phoebe felt Shade's hand muscles flex.

"Don't talk to her," he warned.

"I mean no harm, Shade. Let Phoebe go, and let me take a look at you. I promise I won't touch her."

"Never," he growled.

"I know what you're feeling right now, Shade," Jade went on with a calm voice. "You feel like you want to run away with Phoebe. Your need to make sure she's safe is greater than your need to live. It makes you look at me with blind rage, but I'm not the enemy, and you *know* that. Search your senses. Deep down, you know this."

Shade remained still.

Phoebe barely dared to move. She was still unable to see

his face, but his tense posture, his firm grip on her arm, and clenched knuckles told her he was ready to attack. He'd do anything to save her. That was why the cyborgs were here. She looked at them again, but none of them looked at her. Their focus was on Shade.

"If they aren't yours, how come they're defending you as if they were bound to you?" Phoebe asked Jade.

"They're trained soldiers and it's in their programming to defend anyone that the women they're bound to tell them to defend."

Without warning, Shade lunged at Jade. He grabbed her by the throat and pressed her against the wall. "I said don't talk to her!"

Jade groaned from the impact but didn't get the chance to take a breath before Shade lifted her with one hand. Her feet dangled above the floor and her face quickly turned red when no air reached her lungs. She grabbed his arms, trying to make him let go, but he was too strong.

Rain and Dare reacted immediately. They stormed into the room, grabbed Shade, and forced him away from Jade.

Pain filled Phoebe as she watched them press him to the floor.

Shade tried to get free. He roared again and the deadly look in his shining eyes was intense.

Phoebe's gaze went blurry. Cold chills traveled down her spine as her blood pressure rose.

They weren't hurting him, they just held him down, but the sight almost killed her on the inside. She feared for his life.

Every newborn cyborg went through this but if he didn't get a grip on his possessiveness over her, he'd never be allowed to leave MedAct.

He'd be considered a failure and dangerous.

Dangerous cyborgs weren't allowed to walk the streets. They had to be able to handle other people and other cyborgs being near their bound one.

Shade wasn't doing a very good job so far.

"Is this normal, too?" Phoebe asked when Shade roared a third time.

He pulled all he had but the two cyborgs still managed to hold him down.

"Yes," Jade said and massaged her neck. "Most cyborgs react this way the first time. Don't worry. He'll be given all the time in the world to adapt. If a month isn't enough, you two will have to stay longer. It's as simple as that."

"What will happen if he fails to adapt?"

"We never terminate a cyborg if that's what you're wondering. If one is unable to adapt, we have a way to make sure he'll get a good life, but it almost never happens, and as you know, the cyborgs have been around for about fifty years. They just need time."

Phoebe took a deep breath and nodded. She couldn't let her fears rule. Her gaze turned to Shade, who still struggled on the floor, but not as intensely anymore.

"I see we won't get anywhere today. I'll come back tomorrow and try again. Maybe it will be easier for him then." Jade went to the door. "Rain, Dare. You can let him go."

The cyborg soldiers obeyed and stood. Without another word, they all left the room and closed the door behind them.

Silence surrounded Phoebe and Shade.

She dried her eyes as he rose from the floor. He didn't move from the spot as he watched her. She didn't move either. It felt like minutes passed by before he finally approached. He did it slowly, as if he was afraid he'd scare her. Then, without a warning, Shade fell to his knees and wrapped his arms around her waist.

Surprise washed over her. "What are you doing?"

"I failed you," he said. "I'm so sorry."

"It's … okay." She placed her hand on his head.

It was good he regretted his actions. Hurting someone hadn't been put into his programming. He'd done it to protect her, but that didn't make it all right in this situation.

Thank God they had time.

Shade stood, worry in his eyes. "Am I forgiven?"

She smiled. "Yes, you are."

He relaxed. "Thank you. I'll do a better job defending you the next time the doctor comes by. I will not fail you again."

CHAPTER 9

Shade watched Phoebe's smile disappear.

"What?" she said.

Hadn't she heard him the first time? "I said I'll defend you better the next time the doctor comes by. I will not let her talk to you or touch you. I'll be better prepared and take down the cyborgs if they try anything."

Her jaw dropped open and her eyes went big. "You can't do that."

He frowned. "Why?"

"Because it's wrong. You can't hurt others just because they talk to me."

Phoebe obviously didn't understand what he was trying to do. "I am defending you."

She took a deep breath. "That's *not* defending me. That's locking me away from everything and everyone." She placed her hand on his chest. "Remember the second phase? This is it. You must learn to control this. You must accept that others will always, one way or another, be around me." Phoebe gave him a serious look. "I'm yours and you have nothing to worry about. No other man will touch me the

56

way you touch me, but I *will* talk to other people whether you like it or not."

Everything inside him protested. Keeping Phoebe safe was his main priority.

Why didn't she understand that?

"Others can hurt you." Her logic didn't make sense. Didn't she want him to protect her? Hadn't he done the right thing when he'd pushed the doctor away?

The doctor hadn't seemed surprised by his reaction. Maybe she'd known he'd react like that and why wouldn't he? Jade had spoken to Phoebe. Words could hurt, and he didn't want that to happen to Phoebe. He wanted her to be safe, and if it meant keeping her away from others, then so be it.

Her hand moved to his cheek. "You can't protect me from everything. Pain is a part of life, one way or another."

It was? That just sounded wrong. All the more reason to defend her. "It doesn't have to be. I can keep you away from it."

"If you do, you'll keep me away from living my life, too. I have to support us when we get out of here."

"I can support us, too."

She smiled. "Thank you. I appreciate it."

Silence lingered between them for a while.

"Don't you want me to protect you?" he finally asked.

"I do want you to protect me, but you must learn to do it the right way."

Do it the right way? What other way could there be than

keeping others away from her? That was the only way she'd be safe. "And what's the right way?"

Phoebe smiled. "Be by my side. Hold my hand, love me, but don't hurt anyone unless they're a danger to me. I know you see everyone as a threat right now, but I'll help you see who's a threat and who's not."

Shade frowned. He didn't like that one bit, but for her, he'd do anything.

Even learn to tolerate others.

CHAPTER 10

Phoebe didn't know what to expect the following day when Doctor Jade Silva knocked on the door. She and Shade had talked for hours about what had happened. She'd done her best to explain to him that he couldn't run around and threaten everyone who came near her.

The moment the knock was heard, Shade lunged for the door. He ripped it open, making Jade wince. The long hours of talking seemed to be erased from his mind.

Phoebe hurried to the door and placed her hand on his arm. "Remember what we talked about yesterday?"

He clenched his fists. "I'm defending you."

"I know, but there's no need to scare the doctor. She was the one who created you, along with her team of scientists, remember? Do you also remember me telling you that I've spoken many times with her before you were created?"

His face was carved from stone and his lips were pressed together.

The silence was deafening.

"Fine," he finally said. He turned his gaze to Jade. "You can examine me, but you're not going anywhere near Phoebe."

"Fair enough," Jade said.

Shade grabbed Phoebe's arm and pulled her away from the door.

She didn't protest when he placed her behind the couch on the other side of the room. It was a bit extreme, but at least, he was co-operating. It was one step in the right direction.

He placed himself in the middle of the room, half-turned toward Phoebe as Jade entered. The cyborg soldiers from yesterday were with her, and as before, they didn't say a single word.

Shade pointed at the males. "They stay by the door. If they move a muscle, you'll be thrown out before you can blink."

Jade took a deep breath before she exhaled and turned toward Rain and Dare. "You heard him." She looked at Shade again. "Anything else?"

He grinned. "Aren't you angry?"

She shrugged. "I'm used to this. All cyborgs go through this. Some more than others. Protecting your bound one is your main priority. You just wish her well, but you need to know when to protect her, and when not to."

His grin disappeared. "That is not a discussion between you and me. I only speak with Phoebe about those things."

"Unfortunately, it doesn't work like that. I'm your doctor and I'm the one who makes sure everything is all right with you. You can talk all you want with Phoebe about things, but you must talk to me, too. Remember what I told you yesterday. I'm not your enemy."

Shade's expression darkened. "Get on with your examination."

The doctor pulled out a small box from the bag she had on her shoulder. It was black, and about the size of a book. She pushed a button and it opened.

Phoebe had no idea what she pulled out, but it was some kind of device, no bigger than her palm.

Shade looked suspiciously at it, but after a few seconds, he relaxed and nodded.

Phoebe's lips twitched. He'd realized what the device was, just from looking at it. Sometimes, she envied him for his fast learning capability.

"I need you to remove your shirt," Jade said to Shade.

His shining eyes flashed with anger. "You don't have permission to see me without clothes."

Jade gave Shade a serious gaze. "Listen, Shade. I've seen you naked many times. I saw you as a tiny cell, so can we get on with this?"

Shade approached her in one fast move, and in the next second, he stood face-to-face with her.

The cyborg soldiers moved, but Jade raised her hand.

They stopped.

"That doesn't give you the right to see me without a shirt," he growled.

Phoebe's heart pounded. What if this went the wrong way? "Shade, please do as the doctor says."

He shot her a shocked look. Pain took hold in his shining

eyes. "You want me to undress in front of another woman? You want to let another woman see me without clothes?"

She winced and realization washed over her.

If she told him yes, she'd break his heart and maybe even his trust for her, but Jade needed to examine him. There had to be another way. "Can I do that instead?" Phoebe pointed to the box and looked Jade in the eyes.

"I guess we don't have another choice. It'll take some more time before he'll allow another person to touch him." Jade took a step in her direction but halted and met Shade's angry gaze. "Give her the scanner."

Shade took the box from Jade without touching her fingers and approached Phoebe.

Phoebe took the device. She saw a simple black screen on one side of it, along with numbered buttons. On the other side was a metal plate. "What do I do with it?"

"Place it on Shade's chest, as near his heart as possible with the screen toward you. It has to be against his skin."

Phoebe nodded and met Shade's gaze. "Do you want to do it here or in the bedroom?"

"Bedroom." He grabbed her hand and took her to their room. "There's no way I'll turn my back on any of them."

The bedroom door remained open while Shade placed them near the wall and out of sight.

He took off his shirt and threw it on the bed.

Phoebe inhaled sharply, unable to stop herself from licking her lips. She wanted to lock the door, caress him all over, and forget this peculiar situation but took a deep breath instead. "Now what?" Phoebe asked Jade as she pressed the device against Shade's chest.

"The screen should turn itself on."

She watched the black screen go blue before a few digital buttons in different colors showed up. "It's on."

"Good. Now press the digital buttons in exactly the order I tell you. Don't bother with any other buttons."

"Okay."

The doctor rattled off a sequence, and Phoebe followed it. It took less than a minute and each time she pressed a button, the device made a sound.

Shade stood still and watched her with his powerful gaze the whole time without saying anything.

It was almost too much. It was as if he was making promises, that once they were alone, she'd regret telling him Jade could touch him.

It made her shiver with anticipation.

The device made a different sound.

"You can remove the scanner now and give it back to me."

Phoebe nodded even though Jade couldn't see her.

Shade put his shirt back on.

She turned around to go back into the living room, but Shade grabbed her arm. Without a word, he took the device from her and handed it to Jade instead.

Phoebe took a deep breath. This was going to be a long night.

"Thank you," Jade said to Shade as Phoebe entered the living room.

"What did the device do?" Phoebe asked.

"It scanned Shade. Now, I have to go through the results to see how he's evolving, but I doubt I'll find anything wrong. Just by looking at him, I can tell he's fine."

Apart from the possessive side, that was.

Jade smiled at Phoebe. "Don't look so worried. Everything will be fine. I'll give you a break for the rest of the day, but tomorrow, I *will* come back." She looked at Shade. "We'll start your training then."

He gave her a suspicious glare as he pressed Phoebe to him in a protective embrace. "What kind of training?"

"Socializing you. You can't keep on behaving like this if you wish to enter the outside world."

Shade didn't say anything. He just kept glaring at Jade as she placed the device inside the box, then into her bag. A moment later, she said goodbye and left with the two cyborg soldiers.

Shade approached the door and locked it.

Phoebe tensed when he turned around and looked at her with anger in his eyes.

"I belong to you," he stated and approached her. "Is that somehow unclear to you?"

"No."

"Then why did you want me to be touched by the doctor?"

"Because she was doing her job. She wasn't trying to seduce you. She was going to examine you, to make sure you're all right. For me, that's okay. I can't help you if something is wrong. I can drive a car, but that doesn't mean I can repair it. I can take care of my health and body, but when I break a leg, I have to go to the doctor to fix it. Same goes for you. She's your doctor, your creator, and I trust her. I trust her enough to put your life in her hands. All I want is for you to be all right." She placed her hand on his cheek. "I can love you. I can feed you and take care of you, but I can't fix you if something breaks. Do you understand?"

Shade threw off his shirt again. He grabbed her hands and placed them against his bare chest, making her gasp.

The heat from his body hit her palms. She swallowed as warmth gathered between her legs.

"I belong to you and only you. No one else touches me."

"No one will touch you the way I touch you, but you can't stop people from saying hello to you and shaking your hand."

He frowned. "Shaking my hand?"

"Yes," she said. "When humans greet each other, they shake each other's hands and say '*hello*'. Here, let me show you." She grabbed his hand and shook it lightly. "Hello, Shade." She smiled.

Shade's gaze narrowed.

"You're supposed to say '*Hello, Phoebe*'."

He remained still and silent.

Phoebe sighed. "There are many ways to greet someone, but this is the way we, who live here, do it."

"You allow other males and females to touch you like this?"

"Yes, and you can allow it, too. I won't get angry at you for saying hello to someone."

He went silent again.

She took a deep breath. Thank God they had a month ... or more if needed.

CHAPTER 11

Phoebe stared at the ceiling from the bed. Shade had gone to the bathroom, and she was left alone for a while. It gave her time to think.

Getting Shade to understand the cultural and social things in life wasn't easy. He wanted her to stay away from people to stay safe, but she couldn't do that, and she wouldn't. She'd continue living her life as she had, but she wanted him by her side. Somehow, they would find a way, together.

It's been almost a week since he'd woken up. Jade came by with the cyborg soldiers once a day to help Shade adapt, to help him get used to the cyborg soldiers and her, but progress was slow.

He still didn't let them near her. When they were alone, a lot of their time was spent in bed, and Phoebe loved every minute of it. They got to know each other better. They laughed, cuddled, ate, watched movies, or just talked. Shade was everything she'd wanted him to be.

Only the socialization made things difficult.

Phoebe sat up and grabbed her bag. She pulled out her

cell phone. "Call Faye," she told it and pressed it against her ear while it dialed the number. She heard the familiar beep a few times before Faye answered.

"Hey, girl," Faye said with a happy voice. "I've been waiting anxiously for your call. How are things going?"

Phoebe smiled. "Everything's fine."

"Fine? Then why do you sound so down? Isn't he what you expected him to be?"

"No, he's everything I expected him to be, and more. He's absolutely amazing, and I know you'll love him."

"So what is it?"

Phoebe bit her lip. "We're in the second phase now. I told you about it some time ago. Remember?"

"Yeah, something about socializing him."

"Yes, and I expected it to be difficult, but he's more stubborn than I ever believed he'd be."

"What do you mean?"

"He doesn't allow others to touch me. He thinks they'll hurt me."

Faye chuckled. "Well, you wanted a cyborg and you got one. They're all overprotective when it comes to their bound ones, honey."

"I know, but I never expected him to be like this. I've tried to explain it to him, but he still refuses to listen."

"It's been a few days. You still have a lot of time. As long as you're there for him, I'm sure he'll learn and understand."

Phoebe relaxed. "Yeah, I know. It's just me worrying too much. It will devastate me if I can't take him away from here."

68

"I'm sure you have nothing to worry about."

"I hope so, but it's obvious what we're doing now isn't working."

"And what are you doing now?"

"Shade's doctor, Jade Silva, comes by every day to take a look at him and to talk to him. I don't think he's fond of her. She's straight-forward about everything, and she always has two cyborg soldiers with her that look like mean killer machines. They never say or do anything, but their presence alone makes him tense. Jade said she understands and sees this, but they need to be with her. They are for her own protection."

Faye was silent for a while. "You clearly need another approach. He needs to meet someone else."

Phoebe shifted on the bed and hope awaken within her. "Would you be willing to do it?"

"Hey, you know me. I never back away from a challenge." She laughed.

"You're just as stubborn as he is, and because of that, this might work."

Faye laughed louder. "If he puts on a show, then so can I."

Phoebe grimaced. "Don't say that. We want this to end well, not with an explosion."

"Got it. I could ask Wind and Diane to come with me. It might help."

Wind was a cyborg that didn't live far from her with Diane, his bound one. He was different compared to the two cyborg soldiers Jade always brought with her. He was calm, kind, and gentle, and above all, he didn't look like a killing machine.

"Do you think Diane will agree? Besides, is it wise for her to leave the house now when she's ill?" Phoebe asked.

"Well, I can ask, and if they say no, they say no, but I think Wind would love to help."

She nodded. "Okay, ask them."

"Noted."

"Has anything happened during my absence?"

"No, not much. The neighborhood is calm as usual, but …"

Phoebe tensed. "But what?"

"Scott knocked on your door the other day. I told him you weren't home."

Phoebe winced when she heard Scott's name. The memories flooded her and all she wanted was for them to go away. It was because of men like Scott she'd chosen to apply for a cyborg.

They dated for almost a year and Phoebe got nothing but pain out of it. He hadn't been her first disaster, but he was her last. She refused to experience the things Scott put her through ever again.

He never beat her, but he gladly pointed out she wasn't good enough for him. He'd wanted to change her into something she wasn't, and when she tried her best, and it still wasn't good enough, he hadn't hesitated to tell her so and pull her down with everything he had.

She couldn't recall how many times he'd called her "ugly", "worthless", or "slut". And then there had been all the drinking ...

"Did he do anything?" she asked.

"Apart from being drunk, no. He tried to tell me to open the door, to let him in, but I gave him a piece of my mind and he left."

"He hasn't shown himself for two years. Why now all of a sudden?"

"Well, he was drunk and was probably not thinking. It wouldn't be the first time."

The door to the bathroom opened and closed. Seconds later, her cyborg entered the bedroom.

"Who are you talking to?" he asked.

"My friend Faye."

Shade opened his mouth to say something when Faye's sudden scream interrupted him. "Oh, my God! Is that his voice? You didn't tell me he has such a sexy voice!"

Blood rushed to Phoebe's cheeks when Shade frowned. "He heard you, Faye."

Faye laughed. "Well, then he knows I'm looking forward to seeing him soon. I'll call you back later when I know how things will turn out."

"Okay, bye." She hung up and placed her cell phone back in her bag.

Shade sat down beside her. "Faye is your friend. I have some information about her."

"Yes. She and I have known each other our whole lives.

She means a lot to me even if she can be a little bit too forward sometimes."

He nodded. "You want me to meet her. I heard your conversation when I was in the bathroom."

Phoebe winced. Of course, he'd heard it. His hearing was better than hers. She shouldn't be surprised, but she was. It would take some time to get used to all his cyborg abilities. "And what do you think about that?"

"I guess I will find out when she and I meet."

CHAPTER 12

The tension in the room was like a thick wall. Silence surrounded them, and this could go either way. Shade had been allowed to leave their temporary apartment for the first time; and Jade had brought them into some kind of training room.

It was as wide and as long as a football field with everything from exercise machines to mirrors and open spaces.

No one knew how Shade would react to everything outside the apartment, but so far, he was doing well. At least, when it came to things. People ... well, that was another story. She, Shade, Jade, and the two cyborg soldiers, Rain, and Dare, stood on one of the open spaces.

Her cyborg stood in front of her with his arms open wide while he glared at the two cyborg soldiers.

"Shade, they will only touch her, nothing more and I have already told you a hundred times that I will do it first," Jade said. "You must learn to accept this. It's normal for people to touch each other."

"No. They are not touching her, and neither are you."

Jade looked confused. "We've been going on about this for days now. Most cyborgs understand after a few conversations, but when it comes to you, it doesn't matter what I say, you just don't give up."

Shade didn't say anything. He kept glaring at Jade and the two cyborg soldiers.

Phoebe barely dared to move.

Jade looked at her. Resignation shone in her eyes. "I guess he won't change his mind. When will your friends arrive?"

"Within an hour."

The doctor nodded. "Let's hope it'll work with them. If not, I'll try to find other cyborgs to accompany me tomorrow." She looked at Shade but spoke to Phoebe. "At least, he's letting you talk to me."

She agreed. That was good. Always something.

Jade looked at the papers in her hand. "I guess there's nothing more we can do today. We'll continue tomorrow. You both can stay here and take a look around. It'll do you good, Shade, to start looking at the world from outside the apartment."

She said goodbye and left together with the two cyborg soldiers.

Phoebe didn't blame her for being frustrated. Jade seemed ready for a fight every morning.

Shade looked at all the equipment with uninterested eyes.

They were alone and had about an hour to kill before her

friends showed up.

Worry filled her. What if Shade reacted the same way? There was no guarantee he'd see Faye, Diane, and Wind in a different way.

He'd overheard her and Faye's phone conversation a few days ago. He'd heard her mention Scott, but he hadn't asked a single question about him.

She hadn't given him any information about Scott like she had about Faye. She'd wanted Scott to stay in the past, and there he'd stayed until he'd shown up drunk at her door. Hopefully, it was a onetime thing.

Phoebe gazed at Shade. He was amazing in every single way. When they were together, there was no worry in the world. He was always there for her, always willing to help her with everything.

She'd shown him her work at her laptop, how her marketing business functioned, and he'd figured it out fast. She wasn't meant to work here, but they'd ended up finishing up a few of her projects for her clients.

Everything had gone smooth and faster than usual. Together, they could make her company grow.

But they had to get through this first ...

"Come," she said and reached for his hand.

Shade grabbed her hand, and they walked toward the exit. "Where are we going?"

"I have an idea how to make you relax among people."

He stopped. "I can't be among people yet."

She was glad he respected the rules. "Don't worry. We

won't exactly be among people."

Shade gave her a suspicious look, but he didn't protest when Phoebe led him to the elevators.

She pushed the button and they waited in silence. No one could reach this floor without an approved fingerprint. She'd had her fingerprint approved when Shade had been confirmed for creation.

The risk of meeting someone was slim. Most were inside their apartments getting to know their cyborgs. Phoebe had no idea how many other newborn cyborgs were here at the same time, but she doubted there were many. Cyborgs were expensive, after all.

After almost a minute, the doors to the elevator finally opened, and they entered. It had room for at least ten people. The walls were made of glass and it gave them a great view of what was below.

Shade approached the back wall and looked down.

On the ground floor, they could see the reception area. She'd walked in there just a week ago, nervous but ready to meet him.

And here he was now.

Phoebe pressed the button for the second floor. The doors closed and the elevator headed down.

Her cyborg kept watching the people move around down there. Some headed into the building, some were leaving it. Others stood near the reception, walked in a direction, or talked with someone.

She couldn't tell what he was thinking, but this was his

first time seeing this many people at once. Phoebe counted at least twenty down there.

The reception lobby was huge, wide, and had plenty of open spaces. The big glass windows let through plenty of light to brighten the area.

The elevator stopped and the glass doors opened. They stepped out on a bridge with white floor tiles and glass railings. From there, they had a good view of the reception area. If they met someone, it would be another doctor or another cyborg, and since everyone knew Shade was newborn, they knew to avoid him.

"Do you know why I brought you here?" she asked.

"You wanted me to watch the humans."

"Yes, I want you to see how they interact with each other. I think it might help you understand." Phoebe spotted a perfect example. "Look there, by the plant near the exit. Do you see the blond male cyborg with the woman?"

"Yes," he answered.

A man in a suit approached the couple with a big smile. He shook the woman's hand before turning to the cyborg.

The cyborg smiled and said something.

Phoebe watched Shade. As usual, he was difficult to read, but he studied the people closely. "Look there," she said and pointed to another couple. It was a man and a woman. The woman seemed happy to see the man and threw herself into his arms. "They seem to be close friends, and over there, you have a third example." It was a group of people saying goodbye, with handshakes and waving before they parted.

"Everyone touches each other one way or another." Shade frowned. It was as if he had a hard time believing what he was seeing. "Why isn't the cyborg protecting his bound one?" He looked back at the first couple again.

"Because he knows the man won't hurt her. Do you see any signs of the man wanting to hurt her?"

Shade remained silent for a while. "He is smiling. They are talking."

"Yes. Does that mean he'll attack her?"

Shade met her gaze. "No."

"Exactly. Nothing in his body language indicates that he wishes her any harm."

Shade bit his lower lip. "There is never a guarantee."

Phoebe opened her mouth to answer but shut it again. What could she say to a thing like that? In a way, he had a point, but at the same time, he couldn't walk around and expect everyone wanting to stab him in the back all the time. "You must learn to trust people, Shade. Yes, there are some out there that are bad, but most people just want a normal life and want to be happy. The same thing applies the cyborgs."

"You are talking about the Fighters."

She wasn't surprised. He probably had information about them. "Yes. How much do you know about them?"

"Not much, but I do know they're not bound to anyone. Many cyborgs who lose their bound ones die, but those who survived chose to join the Fighters."

The thought of the Fighters sent a shiver down Phoebe's

spine. They were dangerous, not trustworthy, and they killed without remorse. She'd never met one, but she followed the news. No one knew where they lived, but they showed up in town from time to time, robbing stores for provisions.

No one dared to stop them.

They attacked both humans and cyborgs, and even seemed stronger than regular cyborgs. How that was possible, Phoebe didn't know, but she did know they weren't getting the help they needed.

Instead, they were hunted like animals and killed by the police force. MedAct didn't approve that. For them, each cyborg was important and valuable. They all deserved to live, but not everyone believed that.

"Their leader calls himself Nightmare," she said.

"Nightmare?" Shade raised an eyebrow.

"It isn't his real name, or so I've heard, but he decided to change it after his bound one died."

"Do you know what happened to her?"

"No, but there are rumors."

"What kind of rumors?"

Phoebe took a deep breath. "That she was murdered."

Shade gave her a long look that told her he'd never let that happen to her, that he'd always protect her and be there for her.

It also said he wouldn't let anyone near her.

"Shade, you can't go around assuming it will happen to me. We won't be able to live a normal life if you do. Faye and the others will be here any minute. When they arrive, you'll see there's another side to it all as well."

"What do you mean?"

"As you already know, Faye is an outgoing and happy person. She's looking forward to seeing you. She'll probably give you a big hug to say hello and I'll probably get one, too. Don't push her away. That's just the way she is, do you understand?"

"Phoebe!"

Phoebe looked toward the reception area when she heard someone call her name. She spotted Faye with a huge smile on her face. Phoebe gazed at Shade.

Surprise shone from his eyes.

She couldn't help but smile. Shade had yet to meet anyone as lively as Faye.

Wind and Diane were right behind Faye.

Phoebe waved to them all before she turned to Shade. "Are you ready?"

He answered with silence.

Chapter 13

Shade had no idea if he was ready or not, but he chose to trust Phoebe even if everything inside him screamed to throw her over his shoulder and run away as fast as his legs could take him. His need to protect her was paramount, but when he saw Faye's happy face, he hoped his instincts were wrong.

He and Phoebe returned to their floor. Faye, Wind, and Diane had been granted access for the day. They remained by the elevator and waited for her friends to arrive.

Shade stared at the doors. Any minute now, they would open.

He clenched his fists.

Phoebe placed her hand on his arm. "Relax."

He grabbed her hand and intertwined his fingers with hers. "Stay close to me."

"I will, but don't hurt them if they touch me ... or if they touch you. Promise me that."

Shade clenched his knuckles harder. He didn't want to promise. "I promise."

Phoebe gave him a gentle smile. "Thank you."

It'd slipped right out, and although his emotions told him otherwise, there wasn't much he could do about it. He wanted to protect Phoebe, but he also wanted to make her happy, and that meant doing what she wanted him to.

This was going to be a difficult day.

The elevator doors opened.

An overjoyed Faye jumped out. She made a loud squeak before she came at Phoebe with open arms and with a huge smile on her face.

Shade's instincts took over, and before he managed to think, he pulled Phoebe behind him and stepped forward, glaring at Faye. He tightened his muscles to intimidate her with his tall frame.

She came to a halt and flinched back when she met his gaze.

He looked her over. Faye was a cute female with long, blonde hair, but she barely reached his shoulders. She wouldn't be an issue if she tried anything. Her body was slim, and she didn't look like she weighed much. He could easily remove her if necessary.

Anything to keep Phoebe safe.

From the corner of his eye, Shade saw Wind and Diane leave the elevator.

Wind stopped behind Faye, placed his hand on her arm, and pulled her back. "You are too impulsive, Faye. I told you not to touch Phoebe. Shade is a newborn cyborg, and his instincts to protect her are amplified. It will take some time before he relaxes."

Faye nodded. "Sorry, I forgot."

"Don't worry about it," Phoebe said from behind Shade.

He felt her hand on his arm before she stepped out from where he'd hidden her. He wanted to grab her and place her behind him again where she'd be safe. Not doing so was more difficult than he'd ever imagined, but then he met Wind's gaze.

The cyborg had almond-shaped, metallic-looking eyes, with the color of shining aluminum. Tiny but visible circuits moved around in the iris.

He was almost as tall as Shade was. Wind was fit with broad shoulders and brown, shoulder-length hair. He was dressed in an elegant black suit, almost making him look like a businessman, but there was a calmness in his eyes that Shade hadn't seen before.

He hadn't met many people yet, but he recognized what he saw in Wind.

Wisdom.

He saw a teacher, someone who could help him in a way Jade was not able to. She was good at what she did, but she had a lot to learn when it came to handling a cyborg. Wind on the other hand, in him, Shade saw a friend.

He stretched out his hand as Phoebe had shown him. "I'm Shade."

Wind smiled and shook his hand. "Hello, Shade. I'm Wind, bound to Diane."

Shade looked at Diane. She was beautifully dressed in a long summer dress, high heels, and a thin coat. She looked older than Phoebe. He guessed she was somewhere around forty-five, but she was also not well. Her blue eyes looked tired, and her skin was dry, with a pale tone. Her dark blonde hair hung down her shoulders without any vitality or volume.

She took a step forward and reached out his hand with a smile.

He looked at it for a second before he turned his gaze to Wind.

Wind nodded, still wearing a smile. Nothing in his body language indicated that he'd attack to defend Diane. Instead, Wind seemed to encourage him to touch Diane. "It'd make me very happy if you'd like to greet my bound one."

Shade nodded and shook Diane's hand. Having Wind's approval felt good.

"Nice to meet you, Shade," Diane said.

"Nice to meet you too, Diane."

Shade turned his gaze to Faye, who smiled at him. She stretched her hand toward him, but he didn't move. He narrowed his eyes instead.

Faye cleared her throat. "I know, I know. I made a mistake. Sorry. It won't happen again, but I couldn't help myself." She shrugged. "I was happy to see Phoebe again, and I'm happy to see you, too. Phoebe has barely talked about anything else but you for the last year. It was sometimes impossible to get her to change the subject. She went on and on about what hair color she should give you, or what kind of personality she wanted you to have." She chuckled and gazed at Phoebe. "I must admit it was kind of cute to listen to all that ... and now you're here." She ogled him. "And I must say, she did a damn good job. You're hot." She grinned.

Shade took a step toward Faye. "I don't belong to you. You'll never touch me."

Phoebe came in between them. "Shade, don't mind her. Remember what you promised me. This is the way Faye is."

"Don't worry, Shade," Faye said. "Just because I think you're hot does not mean I'll try to take you away from Phoebe. I know she's your bound one, but that doesn't forbid me from having an opinion about you."

He didn't answer. Faye tested his patience. She was something new, something he wasn't sure about. He'd have a watchful eye on her, just in case, but overall, he found her harmless with her small and cute frame. "You talk too much."

Wind and Diane chuckled, and when Shade looked at Phoebe, he saw her smile. Something he'd said was apparently amusing.

The only one who wasn't smiling was Faye. She looked angry. Good.

That meant she understood they weren't friends.

Shade gave her a dark grin.

CHAPTER 14

Shade watched Phoebe with a gentle smile from where he sat on the sofa that stood inside one of MedAct's dining rooms. It was a bright room with big windows and a clinical interior.

Jade had allowed them to use it instead of their small apartment for Phoebe's friends' visit. Faye and Diane sat by Phoebe's side by the large round table. They laughed, talked, and smiled. Phoebe was happy.

He liked seeing her happy, but there was a sting in his heart that bothered him. It wasn't *him* making her happy. It was someone else. It hurt, even if it shouldn't. He had to get used to this.

It was becoming clearer and clearer with each passing day, but it wasn't easy. Everything inside of him screamed, telling him to get off the sofa and remove Phoebe from this room. The feeling made him clench his knuckles. He forced himself to remain sitting.

The dinner they'd eaten with Phoebe's friends had been exquisite. MedAct's chefs had done an excellent job of preparing the dishes. It had been everything from the first course to the main course and finally a chocolate dessert. They'd served chicken with mashed potatoes and gravy, a dish he'd come to like. In the end, there had been something called coffee.

Shade had watched Phoebe drink it, but it had smelled funny, and after tasting a sip, he'd decided to never touch it again. How Phoebe could drink it, he didn't know. The hideous taste was still on his tongue, even though it'd been over an hour since he'd tasted it.

He'd eaten many times with Phoebe in their apartment, but having others at the dinner table was strange, at first. She'd been close to him the whole time. Most of the time, she'd been sitting on his lap where he'd held her safe. It made him relax, and now, four hours after meeting her friends, things felt better. They wouldn't hurt her. Shade just wished his instincts would understand that too.

Eventually, he'd been able to let Phoebe go and have her sit on her own chair, and it was all thanks to her. She'd never done anything against his will or argued with him about it. She'd allowed him to take things at his pace, and now, he was able to sit on the couch and watch her as she enjoyed some time with her friends.

Wind sat by his side with a soda in his hand. Both of them watched the women interact.

The three women touched each other from time to time while they talked. It was gentle touches, like putting a hand on the other one's shoulder or a hug. Strangely enough, it didn't bother Shade that much. Not when it came to these women touching Phoebe.

Jade's cyborg soldiers, on the other hand, were another story. If any of them tried to touch her, they'd lose a hand or two. They had almost touched her this morning. The memory made his anger boil up, but he took a deep breath to relax.

"It's getting easier, isn't it?" Wind asked.

"What?"

"The possessive feelings over Phoebe. If we had come a few days ago, you would've been glued to her. Now, you're able to watch her enjoy herself from a distance and know she's safe."

Shade nodded without taking his eyes off Phoebe.

"I know what it feels like," Wind said. "I know what you're going through. About fifteen years ago, I was in your shoes. It was difficult, but once I became a part of the human society, I realized this is the way they are. They need each other, just like you need Phoebe."

"I'm starting to understand that."

Wind gave him a smile. "You have nothing to worry about. She created you for a reason. She wouldn't have done that if it hadn't been for love. She *is* over the moon in love with you and she was in love with you even before you were real. She was in love with the idea of you, and now that you're here, she's the happiest woman out there." He took a sip of his soda. "Do you see the shy looks she gives you from time to time?"

Shade smiled. "Yes."

"What does that tell you?"

He grinned now. "That she belongs to me."

"Exactly. You might be bound to her, but she's just as much as bound to you as you are to her. You're everything to her. She doesn't want to go back to the sad and lonely life she had before you came into the picture. She wants to have paradise with you. Some women who can't find paradise with a human male create a cyborg to find it."

Shade didn't say anything. Instead, he saw Phoebe whisper something to Faye. He couldn't hear what, but if he wanted to, he could make himself hear better. He decided not to.

His gaze rested on Diane. She was an attractive woman, even if she wasn't well. Her pale skin, her tired eyes, her slim figure. She kept smiling as if nothing was wrong, but she was not able to hide it. And yet, everyone pretended as if she was fine.

"You're wondering about Diane," Wind said.

Shade frowned. "Do you read minds?"

The cyborg chuckled. "No, but I'm good at reading people. Diane gave me that ability. She's too trustworthy when it comes to people, and because of that, she has ended up in situations that have affected her badly. She wanted a cyborg who would make her see what she couldn't."

Shade nodded. "What's wrong with her?"

"She's dying." Sadness lingered in Wind's voice.

Shade's heart clenched. Losing one's bound one was every cyborg's worst nightmare. "Yes, Phoebe told me, but she didn't say what was wrong with her. Only that there is something wrong with her heart."

Wind took a deep breath. "I'm sorry, but I can't tell you. Diane doesn't want me to talk about it."

He understood. "How long?"

"A few months."

Shade didn't like hearing that. "What will happen to you?"

"I don't know, but Diane says that she has everything figured out. I trust her, so I don't worry, but the thought of losing her ..."

"... Is unbearable," he finished.

"Yes." Wind took another sip of his soda. "Diane refuses to tell me what she's up to. She says she will tell me when the right time comes."

"She should tell you now."

"I know ..."

Shade didn't know what Diane planned for Wind, but he knew what would happen to him if Diane did nothing.

Her death would destroy Wind.

If it didn't kill him, he'd go crazy and end up with the Fighters. They always took in new cyborgs who lost their bound ones.

There was only one way to save Wind, and that was to bind him to another woman. That was, at least, the only thing Shade could think of.

He doubted there was something else Diane could do to help Wind. The problem wasn't finding another woman. The problem was switching the bound one. It was a complicated process that took time, something Diane obviously didn't have, so what was she waiting for?

A loud bang came from the hallway outside the room. A man roared before another bang came. Someone groaned.

Everyone got to their feet and stared at the door.

From the other side of it came more groans of pain. It sounded like it came from several individuals. Were they fighting?

Worry shone in Diane's gentle eyes.

Wind went to her and pulled her into his arms, but his gaze was set on the door.

Faye's eyes were huge as she clenched her knuckles. She seemed unsure of what to do.

Shade's gaze turned to Phoebe. He needed her by his side. Something wasn't right, and his need to protect her took over. He lifted his foot to go to her, but he didn't get the chance before Phoebe took a few fast steps toward him and wrapped her arm around his waist.

It pleased him that she understood, but he needed to find out what was going on. Judging by the sound of groans and growls it wasn't something good. "Stay here," he told Phoebe and headed for the door. She'd be safe inside the room together with Wind.

For a split second, he found it strange that he was ready to hand over his bound one's safety to another cyborg, but on the other hand, he could trust Wind. He'd felt it from the first moment he'd met the cyborg.

"No way," Phoebe said and followed him.

Shade studied her for a second. It would be pointless to discuss with her. It was written all over her face. Besides, there wasn't time. She sure wasn't making it easy for him to protect her. "Fine, but you stay behind me." He opened the door.

A man was struggling on the floor. Three cyborg soldiers tried to hold him down. The man had to be a cyborg as well, considering *three* cyborgs were needed. Three cyborgs were never needed to hold down a human. One was always enough — with only one hand even.

"Let go of me, you bastards! You'll regret this," the cyborg shouted and kicked with his legs, but the cyborgs didn't let him go.

Further down the hallway, Jade stood with two other doctors. A woman and a man.

Jade prepared a syringe, filling it with a clear liquid. A second later, she handed it to one of the cyborg soldiers who held the other one down.

The male took the syringe and stabbed the wrestling cyborg in the chest.

He screamed and his eyes widened. His body tensed before he relaxed with an exhale. His head slumped to the side and he remained still.

Phoebe peeked out from behind him.

Faye, Wind, and Diane joined them when things went quiet.

"What is going on?" Wind asked the doctors.

Jade approached as the three cyborgs got up on their feet. "I'm sorry," she said. "You were not supposed to see this."

Wind's gaze hardened. "Explain yourselves."

The three cyborgs picked up the unconscious cyborg from the floor and carried him away. The two doctors followed them.

"We're not hurting him. We never hurt any of you, but he escaped and almost reached the elevators before we were able to grab him. He escaped again and ended up here," Jade said.

"Who is he?" Shade asked.

"He's one of the Fighters. About eight months ago, he lost his bound one in a tragic accident. She died in his arms, and he completely lost it before he ran away. He didn't die like most do." She took a deep breath. "We searched for him, but the Fighters found him first and took him in. A few days ago, when a group of Fighters robbed a grocery truck, he appeared. Our team of cyborg soldiers managed to get there before the Fighters got away. They caught him ... but the rest fled. He's been in our care ever since." She looked at them with hope in her eyes. "We think we can help him."

"You want to bind him to someone."

Jade nodded. "That's the only way."

"I want to talk to him," Shade demanded.

The doctor winced and stared at him. "What? No. Why would I let you do that? You're newborn and he's unstable.

The last thing we need is for him to get into your head."

"Cyborgs can't read minds."

"That's not what I mean. You still know so little about how the world works. If I let him talk to you, what stops him from filling your head with lies and garbage? He's one of the Fighters! That's what they do. They're not trustworthy and they'd do anything to get you on their side. Do you understand what I'm trying to say?"

He nodded. "Yes, but I won't be alone. Wind will go with me." Shade gave the cyborg a look and Wind nodded in agreement.

Phoebe took a step forward. "I'm coming too." Shade and Wind opened their mouths to protest, but she silenced them by raising a finger. "Don't go there, boys. I'm going, whether you like it or not. I'm not letting Shade go through this alone."

Faye moved forward. "Don't leave me out. I want in."

Diane sighed and stood next to Wind. "I guess I'm going too since Wind is."

Jade stared at them as if she couldn't believe her own ears. "This isn't some kind of circus. None of you can go. Besides, what can any of you do to help him?"

Shade gave Jade a serious look. "If he is one of the Fighters, he won't trust you. The last thing you want is a bunch of doctors and cyborg soldiers near him to gain his trust. You want him to co-operate? Let me talk to him."

Irritation flickered in the doctor's eyes. "You have a point, but he's dangerous. Will you really allow Phoebe to get close to someone like him?"

"No, I won't. That is why you're going to figure something out to make it possible for her to come with me."

Jade looked even more irritated.

CHAPTER 15

Shade opened the door to the interrogation room and entered. Wind was just behind him.

The room was small with white walls and no decorations. Only a table and three chairs stood inside. The cyborg — the Fighter — sat on a chair. He glared at them with hatred in his eyes. He was tied to his seat.

Shade glanced at the one-way window. He was unable to see anything through it but his own reflection, but Phoebe stood in the room on the other side of that window.

Faye and Diane were with her. Jade, along with her cyborg soldiers, were there, too. The soldiers were not just for her protection, but for his as well. If the cyborg tried anything, they'd be inside the room within seconds, but Shade doubted anything would happen.

The Fighter was drugged judging by his saggy sitting position and the swaying with his head. He didn't look dangerous. Instead, he looked sick and dirty. His long, blond hair looked like it hadn't seen a comb in months. His handsome face and dirty clothes needed to be washed. His eyes shone with a hint of aluminum and whispered of a story filled with hate, despair, and love. Love that had been lost and turned into rage and doubt. He didn't trust anyone.

The Fighter placed his elbows on the table and gave them another glare. "And who might you be? You don't look like cyborg soldiers."

"We're not," Shade answered. "We're here to talk to you."

He snorted. "More brainwashing? Go ahead. You won't succeed."

Wind took a step forward. "What do you mean, more brainwashing?"

The Fighter shrugged. "That's all they ever seem to do here. Talk, talk, talk. Over and over again, they try to convince me to bind myself to a woman. They even brought in a cute one, but you know what I told them?" He grinned. "I told them to get lost. I'll never bind myself to a woman again."

Wind and Shade exchanged gazes.

"Why not?" Wind asked.

"Because true freedom is beyond the bond, but I guess neither of you will ever experience that. As long as you stay bound to your bound ones, you'll never know what I'm talking about."

"You almost died when your bound one died." Wind's gaze narrowed.

The Fighter leaned against the chair and exhaled. "Yeah, but that was just *almost*. I'm still here and I can do whatever I want. No bound one to hold me down. I couldn't be happier."

Wind rested his hands on the table. "That's not what I see. I see a broken cyborg, filled with rage and longing. You long for nothing more but to be bound again. It's written all over your face because you remember how good it felt to have someone in your arms every night. To be with someone who loves you so deeply and purely that you can't feel anything but bliss each and every day of your life."

The Fighter growled. "You have no idea what you're talking about."

"Apparently I have. Your expression proves I'm right."

The Fighter lunged up from the chair, making Wind take a few steps back, but his weak body and the chains forced him to sit again. He breathed fast, and for a second, it looked like he might faint. "These damn drugs," he muttered. "They force me to take them to keep me weak."

"It's for your own and other's safety, and you know it," Shade said. "No one is hurting you."

"No, they're not. They're just trying to force me into binding myself to a woman I know nothing about. She was cute, don't get me wrong, but I felt nothing when I saw her. She didn't stir up anything within me."

"She will once you're bound to her."

The Fighter laughed. "And that's why I'll never bind myself to anyone ever again. Don't you see how fake the bond is? You aren't given a choice. From the second you open your eyes, you're in love with the woman who created you, but that doesn't bother you, you poor blind idiots. You just accept it and are happy with it." His smile died

98

and turned into an angry glare. "Do you really think you would've fallen in love with your bound ones if you'd been given the choice?"

"The bond is the only way for cyborgs to live," Shade said, anger growing within him. This cyborg had obviously lost it. How he could dislike the bond this much was beyond Shade. "The doctors had no choice but to bind us to humans. The first cyborgs died because they didn't have the bond."

The cyborg's grin turned dark. "That's what they want you to believe, you fool. Don't you see the bond is their way to control us?"

Shade frowned. "What do you mean?"

"Look at us. We're superior to humans. We're stronger, faster, smarter ..." his grin widened, "*and* we're better looking. Do you really believe the humans would let us roam around the streets without some kind of control over us? The bond is an excellent way to do that. They fill us with all those goody-good emotions like love for someone and call it '*the only way*'. They make us feel good so we can never abandon the bound one, why would we when we have everything we ever wanted served on a golden plate?" The Fighter stared at them both for several long seconds. "The humans have realized pain and fear isn't the right way for total control. Love is, and you two are head over heels in love with your bound ones, whether you want to be or not. You just accept it."

Silence filled the room. Wind and Shade looked at each

other. Shade saw in Wind's eyes what he himself felt.

The Fighter turned everything good around and created a messed up version of something beautiful.

"I feel sorry for you," Shade said.

The door to the interrogation room flung open, making both Shade and Wind start with surprise.

In came an irritated Faye. She glared at the Fighter and stopped in front of the table.

Phoebe came running into the room. "What are you doing?" She grabbed her friend's arm to try to pull her out of the room. "We said we'd stay in the other room."

"I don't give a damn," Faye said without taking her eyes off the Fighter. "Listen here, Mister. I have no idea what the Fighters have made you believe, but you're *wrong*. The bond is the most beautiful thing there can be between a cyborg and a human. My friend is happy because of Shade. I haven't seen her smile the way she does since he came into her life."

The Fighter lifted an eyebrow and ogled Faye from the bottom up. "Well, well. What do we have here? You're even better looking than the cute one they brought in to me. Want to sit on my lap?" He clapped on his knees a few times.

Faye looked taken aback. "You sure are full of yourself."

He shrugged. "Maybe, but I am also free to do whatever I want. I don't have to put someone else before me all the time."

Jade and a cyborg soldier entered the room. She gave

Shade and Wind an apologetic look. "I'm sorry. She just took off."

The Fighter laughed again. "What an audience I have today. I kind of like it, but you can forget I'll bind myself to anyone. Though I wouldn't mind having this enchanting little lady for a few hours on my own. What do you say, sweetheart? Are you up for a round?"

Faye's cheeks turned pink. A spark of desire and temptation filled her gaze. "How about you tell me your name first and I'll think about it?"

"I'll tell you if you tell me yours first," the Fighter answered.

"Faye."

"Nice to meet you ... Faye." He gave her a dark grin.

"Your name?"

"Silver." He turned to Jade. "Can Faye and I get a room now?"

The doctor sighed. "Enough with the jokes. Faye, you aren't even supposed to be in here, remember? Convincing Silver to bind himself to a woman is obviously not going to work. There's no need for anyone to stay here anymore."

"What will you do with him?" Faye asked.

"He'll be transferred to a place where cyborgs like him live. He'll get a good life there, and he'll stay as long as he refuses to bind himself to someone."

They all left the room.

Jade closed the door behind them. She turned to Shade. "Do you understand now what I meant? I know he managed to affect you with his words."

"The only way he managed to affect me was by surprising me with how he thinks. I feel sorry for him."

She took a deep breath. "Good."

Shade grabbed Phoebe's hand and pulled her toward him. When he felt her hand on his bare arm, a pleasant chill went through his body.

He loved this, feeling her touch, and the warmth of her body against his. He'd never grow tired of this. Why Silver didn't want this was beyond him.

CHAPTER 16

Phoebe put down the last t-shirt in her bag and closed it. She straightened her back and smiled. "There, all packed."

She turned around to see Shade standing by the window. He watched the outside world with a serious gaze even if not much was going on.

It was the same thing every day. People and cars passed by as they headed in different directions. He had stood there many times the last few days. Leaving MedAct was becoming more and more real, and today, that day had finally arrived.

"Are you all right?" she asked.

Shade didn't look at her. "He was right, you know."

"Who?"

"Silver."

She gulped. "What do you mean?"

"About the bond."

A cold chill went through her. "What?"

"I understand his point of view, and to him, what he said about the bond, is true. He wasn't lying. He really believes the bond is a curse."

Phoebe stood frozen. She had many times regretted letting Shade talk to the Fighter. He'd changed after that. He'd been thinking a lot, about what, she hadn't been able to tell because he didn't want to tell her. "And what do you think?"

Shade grinned. "Don't look so worried, Phoebe. Just because Silver believes the bond is a curse, it doesn't mean I do."

Phoebe nodded and relaxed. She needed to trust him. "Have you thought about it? What it'd be like to be without the bond?"

"I have evaluated it, but I only have my side of the story. I don't know what it's like to be without the bond, but looking at Silver, I doubt it's a nice life. Even if he'd never admit it to himself, Silver is miserable. Deep down, I think he wants to be bonded again. He wants the safety the bond gave him, but he is stubborn and believes he'll lose his freedom." He snorted and turned to her. "Being bound to you *is* freedom. What he has is not freedom. He has misery, pain. Silver allows his pain to rule him. He's unstable because of it, and that's also what makes him dangerous."

Phoebe smiled but couldn't feel it on the inside.

Shade grabbed her hands. "Deep down, I think the other Fighters are just like him. They're lonely."

"How can you know for sure?"

"I can't be sure, but I suspect. I've gone through the information about them on the Internet, and a lot of it points to that one thing. They're lonely, but they refuse to let go of their freedom. They were lucky to survive when their bonds broke and being bound to another woman means risking the loss of her as well. Do you see their dilemma?"

She nodded. "They choose to suffer, to be lonely instead of bonding themselves to someone again. They don't want to lose their new bound one."

"That's what I believe, but to be sure, I'd need to talk to Silver again."

"I doubt Jade will let you." Phoebe placed her hand on his arm. "Let it go, Shade. Please. Don't let them get in the way of our happiness."

He raised an eyebrow. "Why would the Fighters get in the way of our happiness?" He grinned. "I love you, but your logic is sometimes confusing."

She blushed. She'd obsessed about it again. Her mind went in a direction his didn't.

Shade was just curious. He was a newborn who learned fast, but he still had a lot to learn about the world, and the Fighters were a fascinating subject, because they'd once been in his situation. They'd been bonded to someone they'd loved dearly.

"Their leader, Nightmare, is an interesting cyborg. He was the first to lose his bound one, about forty years ago. When it happened, the entire world went into shock. It had been unheard of, and no doctor expected a cyborg to react the way he did. One day, he'd been a loving and caring cyborg and had turned into a mad killing machine the next day. That's at least what was written in the newspapers back

105

then. People are afraid of Nightmare and I don't blame them. He has no remorse."

Phoebe swallowed. She'd heard the stories about Nightmare, but what was true and what was false, she didn't know, but she knew one thing. The Internet was filled with crap. "Don't judge him based on what's written on the Internet."

"I don't. I'm just informing you of what's being said about him. It doesn't mean I believe it, but I do believe some truth lies within it. He's been filmed many times breaking into places and hurting people. That, he cannot lie about."

There was a knock on the door.

"Come in," Phoebe said.

The door opened and Jade entered. She had her hair put up in a ponytail and a doctor's coat on. In her hands, she held a notebook and a pen.

No big and bad-looking cyborg soldiers were with her this time.

"I see you've packed," she said and approached them.

"Yes, we're ready to go home," Phoebe said with excitement in her voice.

Jade turned to Shade. "How are you doing?"

His face showed no emotions. Shade's eyes were cold and his voice hard when he answered: "I'm fine."

The doctor sighed and wrote something in her notebook. "Don't worry, Shade. You'll get rid of me soon, but you'll have to come back here from time to time during the next two years."

His eyes narrowed. "I don't want to get rid of you. You are my doctor and I need you, but you need to learn how to handle newborn cyborgs. You did nothing to gain my trust. From the start, you showed me I can't trust you."

"I'm sorry about that, but you're the first one who I've not been able to become friends with."

"Or I'm the first one who tells you what you did wrong."

"Think what you want. I came to make a final check-up on you before I follow you down to the reception area to sign you out."

"Nothing has changed since yesterday."

"Good, but this is protocol."

"Fine." Shade removed his T-shirt. "Get on with it."

Phoebe watched Shade as Jade examined him.

It was amazing how far he'd come. He allowed the doctor's touch now, even if he didn't like it.

His need to defend her was still there, though. A stranger had to go through him before they could approach her. Phoebe didn't mind, as long as he didn't take it any further.

Jade placed the device against his chest. It blinked to life and a few minutes later it was over. She pulled it away and looked at it. "It looks like everything is still fine, and you've developed as you should. I believe you're ready to go home. I'll sign you out." She smiled.

Phoebe could barely contain her excitement.

"How will you get home?" Jade asked. "Do you want me to order a cab?"

She shook her head. "That's not necessary. Wind, Diane,

and Faye will pick us up."

Jade nodded. "When will they be here?"

Phoebe looked at the digital clock that hung on the wall. "They should be by the reception area within twenty minutes."

"Great." The doctor wrote something down again before she looked up. "It has been an interesting month, and I look forward to hearing how things turn out for you two within a few months."

"Thank you," Phoebe said and Shade nodded.

Jade left and Phoebe turned to Shade with a wide smile. She felt like a child about to go on an huge adventure. "Are you ready?"

His expression softened, and he caressed her cheek. There was so much love in his beautiful and shining eyes. "Oh, yes."

CHAPTER 17

The doors to the elevator opened. Shade felt the nervousness rise as he took his first step out. He found himself at the reception area of MedAct with Jade and Phoebe, and just a few feet beyond it was the entrance to the building.

That entrance would also take him, for the first time, to the outside world. He still had a lot to learn, but Doctor Jade Silva believed him to be ready enough to handle the outside world.

His possessiveness was finally under control, and he understood how humans interacted. The basics were there. The rest, he'd learn by living and spending time with Phoebe and her friends and family.

Shade looked to his right. Phoebe was by his side. She gave him a comforting smile and grabbed his hand.

They were finally able to start living a life without someone constantly watching over them. Although, he would have to come back from time to time for checkups.

As long as Phoebe was by his side, he was happy.

"This is it," Jade said as they approached the reception.

He'd watched the reception many times from the bridge

just above their heads, but standing here was a completely different experience.

Everything felt bigger and he found himself among humans he didn't know. They walked by him, heading in different directions. Some for the elevators, others for the entrance. Some entered the building, some went for the escalators. Some even looked him in the eyes before they went on with their business.

Shade looked in the direction of the reception. A man and a woman dressed in identical black suits with white bands around the sleeves near the wrists stood behind the desk. The woman stood by a computer and the man browsed through the digital pages of a newspaper.

As they approached, the man and the woman looked up. The woman smiled at him, but he didn't smile back.

His instincts told him to grab Phoebe and keep her close, but he resisted. Neither the man, nor the woman, was dangerous. They were only doing their job, and right now, that job was to sign him and Phoebe out.

"Hello, Doctor Silva," the woman said.

Shade found the woman plain-looking with her dark hair put up in a ball on the top of her head. She wore a gentle makeup and a professional smile along with well-polished nails. Other males would probably find her attractive, but for him, there was only one woman.

His Phoebe.

"Hello, Erin." Jade turned to the man. "Nice to meet you, Alberto."

The black-haired man answered with a nod and a stiff expression. "What can we help you with today, Doctor Silva?" He was tall with a fit body and darker skin.

"I'm here to sign out Shade and Phoebe. It's time for them to go home," Jade said.

Alberto turned his gaze toward Shade and nodded again with a fast smile, but his eyes remained emotionless, professional. "Congratulations," he said before he turned to Jade. "I'll give you the documents to sign."

Alberto put away his digital newspaper and took a step to the side. He pulled up a big black screen attached to the desk. He tapped on it once and it came alive, turning blue with colorful, digital buttons. "Please, put your hand on the screen in front of you," Alberto told Jade.

A black, rectangular, glass screen was attached to the desk. Jade placed her hand on it with spread fingers. A white light came from the screen and disappeared as fast as it turned up. The screen in front of Alberto reacted with a few beeping sounds.

"Do you agree to Shade being signed out?" Alberto asked Jade.

"Yes."

The man nodded and pushed a few buttons. He looked at Shade. "Now, it's your turn. Please place your hand on the screen."

Jade moved away and made room for Shade.

He moved closer and placed his hand there the same way Jade had. The light showed up and disappeared.

Alberto pressed a few more buttons before he looked at Phoebe. "Are you Phoebe Rogers, Shade's bound one?"

She took a step forward. "Yes, I am."

Alberto nodded. "Please place your hand on the screen to finish the signing."

She obeyed.

"Thank you," the man said and gave them another stiff smile. "I will let Erin finish. I wish you a happy life."

"Thank you," Phoebe said as Alberto walked away.

Erin placed herself by the screen. Her eyes were filled with compassion. "Don't mind him. He's always like this. He's happy for you whether you see it or not." She looked at Jade. "You know what to do, Doctor Silva."

Jade smiled. "Of course." She took her place by the screen again, and for a second time, she placed her hand on it, but this time, the light was red. "I hereby approve that Shade, bound to Phoebe Rogers, is allowed to leave MedAct. He has undergone his schooling for one whole month since he woke up, and has proven he can adapt to our society. If I'm wrong, the responsibility is mine. I'm aware of the risks if something goes wrong, and I will willingly accept the consequences if he should fail during the following two years."

"Thank you," Erin said and pushed a few buttons. "All finished. Have a nice day."

Shade tensed and stared at Jade as she pulled her hand from the screen. He hadn't expected that. "What consequences?"

She gave him a faint smile as they walked away from the desk. "If I've misjudged you, I'll lose my job, and I'll never be able to work with cyborgs again."

Shade's eyes widened. "So, your happiness lies in my hands."

"Yes, so don't go and do anything stupid, Shade." They stopped in the middle of the reception area. "But also know this, I'll not allow you to do anything stupid. It's my responsibility to make sure the following two years will work out for you. I'll bring you in if I find it necessary. Do you understand?"

He nodded. "I will not fail you."

"I trust you ... even if you don't like me much."

He snorted. "Who knows, maybe one day we'll be able to become friends."

She grinned. "I hope so."

A movement to his side caught his attention. He turned his head and saw Wind, Diane, and Faye approach them.

Wind and Diane walked forward, each wearing gentle smiles while Faye waved frantically and almost jumped from happiness,

Shade took a deep breath. There was another person he had a hard time getting along with, and apparently, Faye didn't live far away from Phoebe.

Phoebe had assured him Faye never made unexpected visits or would be in their faces. She wasn't like that. She was just filled with energy and always happy.

Faye gave Phoebe a big hug. Three weeks ago, that

would've been a huge problem for him, but he knew better now. He just didn't like Faye touching Phoebe because she was Faye.

As long as she didn't hug *him*, he was fine, but Faye never made any attempts to approach him. Instead, she gave him a nod.

He nodded back. She meant well, and she was important to Phoebe. Because of that, she was important to him, even if he didn't like her. She made Phoebe happy too, and that was what mattered.

Wind and Diane shook their hands. That was also something he'd learned to accept. He still found the gesture somewhat strange, but if that was how people greeted each other, then he'd greet people like that too.

"So, the day has finally come," Wind said. "How do you feel?"

Shade looked toward the big glass doors that would take him outside. "I'm curious."

"That's a good start."

Diane gave him a reassuring gaze. "We'll all be there for you. I know what you're going through. Some things will be more difficult than others but both Wind and I will help you out the best we can."

Shade trusted Diane. He saw her as a friend, just as he saw Wind as a friend. Besides, Diane had experience when it came to living with a cyborg. She knew what awaited him and Phoebe because Wind had once been in his shoes. With Phoebe and his friends by his side, Shade was sure things would work out just fine.

Jade didn't need to worry about her job.

From the corner of his eye, he noticed more movement.

Silver entered the reception area from the elevators.

Two cyborg soldiers walked by his side, holding his arms in firm grips.

The cyborg soldiers were created to deal with difficult cyborgs because no human could physically take down a cyborg. The cyborgs that held Silver were muscular like bodybuilders, around seven feet, and had fierce facial expressions.

Silver didn't fight them. He was probably still weak and drugged. Also, the handcuffs on his feet and wrists would make it more difficult for him to escape.

"What is he doing here?" Phoebe gasped.

"He's being transported to the place where cyborgs like him live," Jade answered.

"What kind of place is that, exactly?" Shade asked without taking his gaze off Silver.

"I'm sorry, but I can't tell you. That is classified information, but don't worry, he won't be hurt in any way. He'll be well taken care of and will be given a good life, and if he chooses to bind himself to a new bound one, he'll be able to leave."

Shade's gaze narrowed. "He doesn't seem willing to go."

"Of course not. He knows his only way out of that place is by binding himself again and that is the last thing he wants."

Silver noticed them.

Shade met his gaze, and the cyborg gave him a dark grin. There was something in his eyes that Shade didn't like. Silver tried to pull his arms free from the cyborg soldiers' grip, but he wasn't really trying, he was just having fun. It was almost as if he was play-acting ... toying with the cyborg soldiers.

Something wasn't right ...

"Don't worry," Silver told him with a loud voice. "It'll be over soon." He winked.

Phoebe tensed. "What's he talking about?"

Shade opened his mouth to answer, but before he got the chance to say a word, an explosion went off in the reception area.

The blast knocked everyone to the floor, covering them with shattered glass. Within seconds, the calm and elegant reception area turned into a chaotic place with glass splinters everywhere.

The main entrance was destroyed. The glass doors were no more. Several humans lay motionless on the floor, probably dead. Blood smeared the walls, spattered the glass shards, people, and was in growing puddles under some of the bodies.

Shade heard men and women screaming. People ran away from the danger.

His body hurt all over. He groaned from the pressure in his head and the growing headache. It felt like he'd been hit by a wall, but it didn't matter how much his body ached. His only thought was of Phoebe.

Shade grimaced as he tried to get up. A sudden, sharp pain hit him when he tried to support himself on his right hand. He turned his arm. A big piece of glass was sticking out of it.

He sat on his knees and without hesitation, he pulled it out. Somehow, he managed to hold back his scream. His body trembled from the agony, his eyes watered, and his head spun, but he didn't have time for this. It didn't matter how much he hurt. He had to check on Phoebe. She was in danger.

Diane sat on the floor with messy hair and glass splitters on her clothes, but she seemed unharmed. Wind was by her side. He held her in his arms wearing a stern facial expression. Apart from a few bleeding scratches on Wind's arms, he seemed fine, too.

Jade was already on her feet, looking around with a worried gaze.

Phoebe, on the other hand, lay on the floor.

Motionless.

"No," Shade gasped and crawled to her, ignoring the pain in his body.

He grabbed her shoulder and turned her on her back. With a quick glance, he looked her over.

Glass splitters lay on her clothes and in her hair, but there was no indication that she was injured. Confusion struck him. She was breathing as if she was sleeping.

He shook her lightly, but she didn't wake. Then he noticed something white sticking out from her leg. Shade grabbed it and pulled it out.

A dart.

"What the—" His confusion rose.

"Bad aim. Sorry about that. It was meant for you."

Shade jerked around and stood, making the ache in his body grow, but the familiar voice told him he shouldn't show weakness. He tensed, staring right into the eyes of Silver.

The Fighter grinned. "I won't miss this time."

Shade heard a muffled sound, and a sharp stinging pinched his stomach. He jerked from the pain, groaned, and looked down. A dart, similar to the one he'd pulled out of Phoebe, was in his flesh.

Silver pointed a gun right at him.

Phoebe's dart that Shade held in his hand fell to the floor.

"That's better." The Fighter's grin widened.

Silver's cuffs were gone. The two cyborg soldiers that had been by Silver's side lay still on the ground. Had Silver taken them down? And where had he gotten the dart gun from?

He heard the chaos around him. The screaming and running still went on. People fled for their lives, most aimed for the damaged entrance to get away. What was going on? It'd all happened so suddenly.

Shade pulled the dart from his stomach. It didn't take long for his body to weaken from whatever it'd been dipped in. His knees wobbled, almost unable to hold him up. "What are you doing?" he asked with a shaky voice.

"What has to be done."

Despair filled him as he watched cyborgs dressed in

118

black, carrying heavy guns storm the reception area. He recognized one of them. The sight of the cyborg sent chills down his spine.

Nightmare.

The leader of the Fighters.

He was a tall, muscular, dark cyborg with nasty looking shining eyes. The scar on his throat didn't ease the frightening and maddening impression of him.

Anger rose within Shade as Nightmare locked gazes with him. No one was going to hurt his Phoebe. He'd fight to defend her, protect her.

Dizziness filled his head, his sight became blurry, and his knees finally gave in beneath him. He fell to the floor, hurting his injured arm in the process. He groaned with pain but didn't let it stop him from crawling closer to Phoebe, shielding her with his body.

Nightmare stopped in front of him with a pleased smile. "Don't worry, Shade. Everything will be all right."

Shade glared at the cyborg as confusion sang inside him. "What do you want? How do you know my name?"

"I know everything."

His eyelids felt heavy, so heavy … His body was even heavier as each muscle relaxed. He wanted to sleep … needed to sleep …

No. He had to protect Phoebe.

He looked at her, placed his hand on her in a desperate attempt to keep her away from Nightmare.

"Sleep now, Shade," Nightmare said.

Shade's head slumped to the side. Darkness took him.

CHAPTER 18

Shade opened his eyes and jerked to a sitting position. His heart pounded like crazy as he frantically looked around for Phoebe, but all he saw was a big bedroom.

He sat on a king-size bed with white linens. The walls were painted in a bright yellow, and in front of him was a big window, going from the floor to the ceiling, letting in gentle sunlight. Thin, white curtains decorated the window.

To his left was an open door, and next to it, stood a wide wardrobe with glass doors. Next to the bed sat a cute but unfamiliar woman on a chair, reading a book.

She gave him a surprised look, flew up from the chair, and headed for the door. The woman stopped in the doorway, leaning her head out. "He's awake!" she yelled out before she turned and approached him.

"Who are you?" He glared at her. "Where is Phoebe?"

If Phoebe was hurt, someone was going to regret it.

"Relax, Shade. You're among friends."

The woman was tall with a slim figure. Her hair was light blonde and in a ponytail. She reminded him of a doll with her cute and innocent-looking face. Her green eyes radiated kindness and love, but also shyness and insecurity. And yet, the woman seemed highly intellectual.

He looked at the book she'd been reading. The title read, "Cyborgs and Science". "Who are you?" he asked again, this time with a colder voice.

The woman swallowed. "I'm Celise. I'm a friend of Phoebe's."

When he heard Phoebe's name, his mood darkened even more. Shade pushed the cover aside and stood.

An image of Phoebe, lying hurt somewhere, crossed his mind. That triggered his anger, making him tighten his muscles to the point of pain.

Celise's eyes widened as he approached her like a hunter approached its prey. She gasped and took a step back.

He'd make the woman talk. He wouldn't hurt her, but he could use fear to make her tell him everything she knew. "What have you done to Phoebe?" he growled.

"I haven't done anything. I'm her friend. Didn't you hear what I said?"

Shade's rage was too great for him to care. He had no idea where he was, but he remembered what had happened before he'd passed out.

Nightmare, the leader of the Fighters, had leaned over him.

That could only mean one thing.

They had taken him.

This place had to belong to the leader, and this Celise was a part of his gang. The fact she was human didn't stop him from coming at her.

The sound of running feet came from outside the room. It made him turn his focus to the half-closed door.

He clenched his knuckles. He would fight anyone who came through that door. They'd regret ever taking him away from his Phoebe. He was ready. He'd be the first one to strike. He'd take them by surprise.

The door opened wide.

Shade lunged. His body tensed, ready for a fight.

Wind, Diane, and Faye entered.

He jerked to a halt. "Wind?"

Wind smiled and approached him. "I'm glad to see you're finally awake. You've been out for hours."

Shade looked around at the people in the room. He blinked at seeing *them,* instead of Nightmare, but he didn't see Phoebe. "Where am I?" His gaze returned to Wind.

"This is Phoebe's home ... your home."

Shade winced. Phoebe's home? *His home?*

He took a quick glance around again and found the room's interior delicate but appealing. On the other side of the room was a white bookshelf. On it stood plenty of colorful books. There was also a framed photo of her. Phoebe.

His Phoebe.

Shade's anger returned. "Where is Phoebe?"

Wind's smile faded. "You'd better sit down and I'll explain everything."

Without wasting another second, Shade sat on the bed.

Wind took a seat next to him, while Celise, Faye, and Diane found chairs next to the bed.

"What's the last thing you remember?" Wind asked.

"Nightmare leaning over me and the Fighters storming the reception area."

"They did, but they didn't take it. MedAct's cyborg soldiers came to the rescue within a minute and managed to take the Fighters down. Some were arrested but most fled." Guilt filled Wind's eyes. "I couldn't help you or Phoebe. You were both out of my reach and Diane was my priority."

Shade nodded. "I understand. She is your bound one and the bound one comes first."

"We got to safety, thanks to Jade. She has access to MedAct as few do but watching what went on behind safe doors was almost worse. The cyborg soldiers did everything to protect you and Phoebe from harm, but they barely had the chance to move you before the Fighters were all over them." Wind frowned. "It was as if you and Phoebe were the Fighters target." He met Shade's gaze. "They came for you and her."

Silence filled the room. The tension grew so thick, it almost became difficult to breathe.

He stared at them.

They all had sadness in their eyes, even the unknown female, Celise.

She peeked at Wind from time to time. There was something else in her eyes as well, something he couldn't place.

"They took her," Shade said, his focus returning to the situation.

Wind nodded. "They did. She was the easier target."

The pain in his heart shredded him up on the inside. Every cell in his body screamed with despair and frustration. He had to make her safe again.

If Nightmare hurt her, he'd pay with his life.

A dangerous cyborg was not to play around with, and right now, Shade felt deadly.

"Why?" he growled. "Why did they take her?"

"We don't know," Faye answered, "but it was obvious they wanted you first. When they didn't succeed, they went for Phoebe."

"What did Nightmare and Silver say to you?" Diane asked.

"Not much, but their words didn't make sense. Nightmare told me everything would be all right and Silver said he was doing what had to be done."

Everyone looked at each other.

"They are up to something," Faye said. "They must've had an eye on you and Phoebe. I don't know how, but I heard Nightmare say your name, Shade. He *knew* you."

Shade nodded. "Yes, he did say my name."

"That's worrying," Diane said. "Jade should be here. She needs to hear this."

"Why isn't she here?" Shade asked.

"The Fighters ruined the entire reception area. Thankfully, they didn't get far, but they did a lot of damage.

124

Many cyborg soldiers got hurt and Jade had to stay behind to help."

"Of course. Why was I brought here?"

Wind answered. "MedAct isn't safe right now. Besides, you'd been signed out and you're no longer their responsibility. Jade believed you'd be safer here. Glaswell is a protected town behind high walls. No one can get in without permission."

Shade could only nod. Everything within him screamed for Phoebe. He wanted to shout his anger and frustration, but held it in.

"We have to do this on our own," Faye said.

Everyone looked at her.

"Do what?" Diane asked.

"Save Phoebe of course! Do you expect us to just sit around and do nothing while Phoebe goes through God knows what?"

Diane's gaze darkened. "No, I do not, but what can we do?" She looked at the others.

"We have to find the Fighters," Wind said, "but their location is unknown."

Celise raised her hand and blushed when everyone looked at her, especially when Wind met her gaze.

"Yes?" Wind asked with a gentle smile.

She reddened even more and looked down. "Well ... um ... I have an idea." She looked around. "As you all know, I've been studying cyborgs for many years, and what I discovered lately, might help us get Phoebe back."

125

That got Shade's attention. "What did you discover?"

"The Fighters have been out there for forty years, ever since Nightmare lost his bound one, but no one has ever been able to locate them. I think it's because no one ever thought about connecting the cyborg's vibrations."

"What do you mean?" Diane asked.

Celise's eyes shone with excitement as she explained. "There's a signal within every cyborg. It connects them. A universal signal. It's mentioned in almost every book about cyborgs I've read and I'm sure you're both aware of it." She gave Wind and Shade a look, and they nodded. "As you also know, it wasn't intentionally created by MedAct. They discovered it sometime after the first cyborgs were created, so deleting it was out of the question. The signal was already a part of the program that makes a cyborg a cyborg. Taking it away is like taking away a human's heart, so MedAct just left it there. It's harmless; at least, they seem to think so, but there's almost no information about it. All the books ever say is that it links the cyborgs together, and how it was discovered. No one seems to have considered that the signal can be used for more ... a lot more." She gave them a longer look and straightened her back. "I discovered it can be used to track down a cyborg."

Faye frowned. "So, what you're saying is—"

Celise's eyes shone even brighter as a wide smile decorated her pretty face. "If I can pinpoint the signal through one of you," she looked at Shade and Wind, "I can track Nightmare down and give out his exact location. That way, we can find Phoebe."

Shade flew up onto his feet. "Do it."

Celise winced. "Now?"

"We have no time to lose."

Wind stood and placed a hand on Shade's arm. "Wait, Shade." He turned to Celise. "Are you sure the process is safe? The last thing we want is to injure Shade."

"Maybe we should call Jade," Faye suggested.

"I've studied the signal for some time now and nothing indicates that it's dangerous. I don't know what it will feel like though," Celise said.

Wind nodded and looked at Shade. "It's your choice."

Shade took a deep breath. "I'm ready."

"What about Jade?" Faye asked.

"There's no time," Shade said. "Phoebe is in danger."

Celise left the room for two minutes. She came back with a small laptop in her hands that she placed on the table. Green holographic images of some kind of device arose from it when she pressed a button.

Shade studied them and nodded to himself when information about the device filled his mind.

It was an advanced search program designed to wirelessly connect with a cyborg's hidden signal.

Celise gave him an uncertain smile.

"You created that program," he said.

"Yes, I thought it might come in handy. I have MedAct's medical license and I help cyborgs with technical issues. I studied at their school for many years, but the dream is to

127

one day do what Jade does." She got a dreamy look in her eyes. "I'd love to be a part of the creation process."

"You should talk to Jade about it."

She licked her lips. "I still have a lot to learn." Celise pushed a digital button on the computer screen, making the holographic device react.

"Don't be shy, Celise. You know a lot already. You know more about me than I know about myself, and I'm the cyborg," Wind said with a smile.

Celise's cheeks turned pink.

"You want to create your own cyborg, don't you?" Shade asked.

She stopped what she was doing and glanced at Wind. The pink on her cheeks turned red.

He'd seen that look in her eyes before. It was there whenever she looked at Wind.

Of course. He understood now.

It was longing and desire.

"No," she answered and continued with her program.

Shade glanced at Wind.

The cyborg gave him a knowing look.

Shade glanced at Diane and saw the same understanding and awareness in her eyes. She knew too.

They all knew.

A short silence followed.

All that could be heard was the tapping of digital buttons on Celise's laptop.

"There, it's ready," she finally said. Shade approached her

as she grabbed the chair she'd been sitting on and indicated for him to have a seat. "As I said, I have no idea what it will feel like. It might hurt, it might not. The signal is buried deep inside your program so I assume there will be some kind of sensation. It shouldn't take more than a few minutes for me to locate Nightmare ... if everything goes as it should. If you want to interrupt, just let me know and I'll stop."

Shade nodded and prepared himself. He expected this to hurt a lot, but he'd do this, for Phoebe.

She was out there somewhere, and she needed him.

He needed her.

The hole in his chest grew with each passing minute, filling him with loneliness and despair. He couldn't help but wonder if this was what cyborgs who lost their bound ones felt, but for them, it was probably a lot worse.

"Are you ready?" Celise asked.

He turned his focus to her. "Yes."

"Good." She pressed a button. "I will begin ... now." Celise pressed another button.

Shade tensed. He clenched his knuckles and waited for the pain, but it never came. Instead, he felt a tingling in his head.

Celise focused on her laptop, pushing keys and spinning the holographic device. Her expression was serious and determined. She seemed to know what she was doing, and that gave him hope.

Maybe this would work.

Wind moved restlessly where he sat on the bed. "I feel

a strange sensation." He shook his head, as if to get rid of something.

Celise stared at him. "I'm not doing anything to you."

"What exactly are you feeling?" Shade asked.

"Like thousands of ants are running around inside my head. It's not painful, but it's not comfortable either."

"That's exactly what I'm feeling."

Both cyborgs looked at Celise.

Realization flashed in her eyes. "Damn it!" She returned to her program, pushing buttons like never before.

No one dared to say a single word. The minute that followed felt like hours.

"I got him!"

A few more keys were pushed before the holographic device disappeared along with the tingling sensation inside Shade's head.

She leaned back in her chair, giving a big exhale. "That was close."

"What just happened?" Faye looked confused.

"Remember I said that the signal connects all cyborgs?"

"Yes. So?"

Celise pulled her hand through her hair. "Well, now all cyborgs know that something was being done to one of them. I didn't connect to Wind, and yet, he felt everything. Meaning, every cyborg out there felt it. I didn't expect this to happen. I thought the chance of it happening was slim. I wouldn't be surprised if MedAct also caught that the signal was being tampered with."

Diane gasped. "That's not good."

Celise looked down at the floor and curled up. He cheeks turned pale.

Wind rose from where he sat and approached her. He placed his hand on her arm and flashed a gentle smile. "Don't worry. Most cyborgs will not know what happened. All I felt was a tingling inside my mind, and figuring out what caused it, will take time. Many will not even pay much attention to it."

Celise looked up at him with gratitude. "Let's hope so."

"You said you found Nightmare."

"Yes, I found him."

Wind's gaze turned serious. "Where is he?"

CHAPTER 19

Phoebe opened her eyes. Her body was so heavy. It was as if she'd been drinking all night, and now she had to face the consequences.

The brain fog didn't let go easily, and all she wanted was to go back to sleep, but when she managed to look around with her gritty eyes, it dawned on her she wasn't where she should be.

The light inside the unknown room was dim, and it took a while to register her surroundings. The last thing she remembered was a sting in her leg. After that, there was nothing, and now, she was here. Wherever *here* was.

She sat up on the bed and looked around.

The room was in desperate need of renovation. The wallpaper was decorated with heavy patterns in a sharp yellow color. A worn lamp hung from the ceiling, and yellowish curtains covered the only window. The bars in the window made her tense.

There was a rundown, wooden wardrobe next to the door, and mold grew in one of the corners. Phoebe wrinkled her nose as disgust filled her. The air felt almost warm and moist. The room desperately needed a good airing, but the window looked like it was sealed tight.

At least, the linens were fresh and clean.

Phoebe jerked when the door opened.

The Fighter Silver walked in and smiled as he approached the bed, but the gesture didn't reach his eyes. "You're finally awake." He sat on the bed. "We've been waiting for you to come around. I guess the dose was too strong for you. It was meant for a cyborg, but I managed to hit you first. Sorry about that." He didn't look sorry one bit, though.

Phoebe glared. "Where am I?"

"Somewhere far away from your cyborg, but don't worry. We'll stay here until he finds you. In the meantime, make yourself at home. Do you want some coffee? I was thinking of making some for myself."

Was he serious? Nothing about him told her that, though.

"Not thirsty?" he asked.

Phoebe put some more threat into her voice. "Where. Am. I?" She wouldn't let him intimidate her. Sure, he was a scary, but hot, looking cyborg with his muscular frame and sharp gaze, but she was an angry human woman.

"My, my. And here I thought Faye was the one with an attitude. I guess you don't show yours often, do you?"

"Are you going to answer the question or not?"

Silver stood, wearing a grin and approached the window. He pulled back the curtain. "Take a look yourself."

Phoebe's tension grew, but she joined him at the window,

not lowering her suspicion. She had no idea what she'd see, but something told her she wouldn't like it.

Her heart fell when she was greeted by the sight of nothing but sand and a few dead bushes here and there, as far as the eye could see. "Are we in the middle of a desert?"

"You could say that, so there's nowhere to escape. Remember that. You can run, but you'll die from starvation or thirst long before you manage to reach any civilization."

Her heart fell even further. How was Shade going to find her out here? Tears gathered in her eyes, but she pushed them away. The last thing she wanted was the bastard to see her cry.

Sure, he was huge, but he didn't scare her, well only a little. Besides, something told her he wouldn't hurt her. He needed her.

If she wasn't mistaken, this was the desert located about three or four hours outside of Glaswell. About a hundred years ago, the area had been filled with trees and life. Now, this wasteland was all that remained, and sadly, it stretched on for miles and miles.

"Why am I here?"

"I think you already know."

She bit her lip. Yeah, she knew. "It's not me you want. You want Shade. Why?"

Silver grinned. "Why don't you smile a little? That serious face of yours doesn't suit you. Your friend Faye was, at least, more interesting to talk to. She had some spirit. I wouldn't mind talking to her again."

Phoebe snorted. "I doubt Faye wants anything to do with you after the way you flirted with her last time."

His grin returned as he shrugged. "Well, that's the only thing I can do lately. Your friend Faye is hot enough to have a few steamy hours in the bed with, but that would trigger a bond, and that's the last thing I want."

She winced. "You can't have sex?"

Silver raised an eyebrow, as if he was surprised she didn't know that. "No, I can't touch a woman. If I do, my bond will think I want to bond with her, and it will initiate the bonding process."

Phoebe stared at him. Somehow, it hadn't hit her that the Fighters had to give up sex and nearness to another person to stay unbound. "Not even a kiss?"

He shook his head. "Nope. Not even a kiss. No touching, but I can flirt with women all I want. It's fun." Silver winked.

Phoebe snorted. "You must be lonely."

That wiped the grin off his face and his eyes darkened. He took a step closer to her. "I'm not lonely."

"Yes, you are. That's why you're flirting with women. It's why you're such an arrogant prick. I see right through you, Silver, and I believe the things Shade and Wind told you at MedAct. You wish you were bonded again because you don't want to be alone, but you're afraid to bind yourself to a woman again because you fear you'll lose her, too."

He growled. "You know nothing about me."

"Your defensive mode tells me otherwise."

Silver grabbed her, making Phoebe gasp. He looked

135

pissed. Angering him was not the smartest thing, but thousands of emotions lingered inside her. Everything from despair to confusion.

She wanted to get away from here. She wanted to get to Shade and make sure he never came here. Whatever the Fighters wanted with him couldn't be good.

"Let her go!" a deep voice boomed from the door.

She and Silver whirled, staring right into the eyes of a furious Nightmare.

Before she got the chance to react, the huge and intimidating Fighter lunged. He grabbed Silver by the throat and threw him against the wall.

The whole room shook from the impact, making it feel like a small earthquake.

Silver grimaced and groaned with pain.

Phoebe stared at the scene taking place in front of her with huge eyes. She backed away, as not to get in between them.

The crazed look in Nightmare's eyes as he pressed his fingers tighter around Silver's throat told her he meant business. He would snap Silver's neck if he wanted to. "I told you not to touch her," he growled.

"I wasn't going to hurt her." The blond Fighter struggled to get free, but Nightmare was too strong for him.

"I don't give a shit what you think you were not doing. I told you to stay away from her, but you didn't listen. She's not one of your toys to play around with. She has a bound one. You will respect that. Now, get out!"

He pushed Silver out from the room and slammed the door behind him.

Phoebe pressed herself against the wall as Nightmare turned toward her with a glare that would kill if it could.

The black-haired Fighter flashed his teeth and gave out an animalistic snarl. There didn't seem to be much sanity left in him.

She could be bitchy with Silver, but with *this* Fighter, that would be an awful idea. He was fierce, deadly, and dangerous like no other. He was also the first of the Fighters; he'd had plenty of time to lose his mind. He'd been without a bound one for about forty years, and after watching his actions in the media, he had little regret.

Nightmare killed without remorse and robbed places without a second thought. He could kill *her* in the blink of an eye.

Without a word, he came at her.

Phoebe couldn't help the squeak that escaped her lips when he invaded her personal space.

He locked her between his arms and placed his palms against the wall on each side of her head.

She barely reached to his shoulders, and he seemed twice as wide as her. He could break her neck without much effort.

Phoebe expected him to threaten her with all kinds of awful things. But to her surprise, he did the last thing she'd expected him to do.

His facial muscles relaxed as he exhaled and leaned his head against the crook of her neck. His heavy body pressed against hers and he cuddled himself against her. Nightmare's body heat surrounded her and his appealing and masculine scent filled her nose.

Phoebe was unable to move, but it felt like her heart would explode out of her chest. What the heck was he doing?

"Just a little while," he mumbled against her throat. "Please ... let me stay like this for a little while."

His words stunned her. "What?"

She felt him press his lips and nose against her as if he was breathing her in. He didn't kiss her, but his lips brushed her skin, sending goosebumps all over her body. And when he pressed his big, muscular body even closer, Phoebe was ready to fight for her life, but she remained still.

Nightmare didn't move. He just remained like that, snuggled up against her. He didn't say anything either.

All she could hear was his silent breathing.

"Don't be afraid, Phoebe. I won't hurt you. I just need to feel ..." His words were a whisper, but he didn't finish his sentence.

"Nearness to someone?" she suggested with a gulp.

He nodded against her neck. "Yes. I need it so much. You have no idea what it's like to be alone for so long. My bond tells me to find a woman to bind myself to. It screams inside of me like crazy every single day, driving me mad."

"Silver said you can't touch a woman without binding yourself to her." Fear gripped her. The last thing she wanted was this dark and intimidating cyborg bound to her.

"That is true. Intimacy will tell my bond I want a bond with her, but I can't bind myself to a woman who already has a cyborg. My bond recognizes that you are not available and will not initiate the bonding process. You're safe ... and so am I."

Confusion struck her. "You are safe?"

"Yes. You can give me this moment of intimacy without me risking binding myself to you. Don't worry. I will not touch you in an inappropriate way. I just ... want to stay like this for a little while."

Nightmare went silent again, and Phoebe had no other choice but to let him lean against her. She heard his steady breathing and felt the heat from his skin against hers as the minutes passed by.

He seemed to be relaxing, but she remained tense. She worried he'd suddenly switch back to the dangerous Fighter she'd seen when he'd entered the room.

"You told Silver not to touch me, to respect that I have a bound one, and yet, you are touching me yourself."

"I'm respecting you," he answered. "Silver would have toyed with you. That's what he does to get his fill of nearness."

"And you turn to women with bound ones."

"No, I rarely get the chance, because most of them live in Glaswell. They're out of my reach. The women I encounter don't belong to a cyborg. They belong to a human male, and human males don't count. My bond approves those women as potential bound ones. It tells me they are accessible."

She couldn't help but feel pity for the Fighter.

He wasn't crazy. He was lonely. Desperately.

"Why do you fight a bond so much?" she asked.

"Because it's not real."

Phoebe swallowed. "What Shade and I have is real."

"Yes, for you it's real. I don't doubt that, but Shade never had any say in it. From the moment he woke up, his bond told him he was bound to you, that he loved you, and *why* would he question it? You make him happy, and that's all that matters. But once you lose your bound one, you realize how fake your life has been. MedAct makes you believe they bound you for your own survival's sake and that cyborgs can't exist without the bond." He raised his head and looked her deep in the eyes. "I say they plant it inside us to control us. We function just fine without it."

Phoebe's chin trembled. His shining eyes with the black pupils were mesmerizing and frightening at the same time. "But most of you die when the bond is broken."

"Yes, MedAct made sure of that too."

Maybe she'd been wrong about him. Maybe he was crazy after all.

"Do you have any proof of what you are saying?"

"Just my own past, and every Fighter that stands with me. They experience the same."

"That is not enough. No one will listen to you."

"Not yet, but we *will* get there one day."

Phoebe frowned. "So, what do you need Shade for?"

"He's a newborn cyborg. We hope he'll be able to help us

solve the biggest riddle of them all."

"And that is?"

Nightmare remained silent for a while, just looking at her, never moving away. "How to free a cyborg from his bound one without killing him."

CHAPTER 20

"I'm going!" Faye yelled at Wind. "Phoebe is my friend. There's no chance in hell I'm staying here to sit around and wait for you and Shade to come back."

Shade saw irritation in Wind's eyes, but the cyborg remained calm.

"We have already discussed this, Faye. You can't go," Wind said. "You will only be in the way. Besides, what can you do to help? The Fighters are huge and mean cyborgs. To them, you're easy prey."

Faye glared at Wind, with her hands on her hips. "I don't give a damn what you think. It's not your call."

"Yes, it is. Only Shade and I are going. We're the ones who have a chance against the Fighters. They took Phoebe for a reason, and that reason is to get Shade to come to them. It will be dangerous. Too dangerous for a human woman. You don't have the strength to fight off a Fighter."

Shade and Wind stood packed and ready to leave in the hallway to his and Phoebe's house, along with Faye, Celise, and Diane. Nightmare and his Fighters were hiding somewhere outside of town, in the wastelands.

He had no idea what awaited them, but Shade was prepared to face whatever came his way. He had to get Phoebe back.

Faye looked at Diane with anger written all over her face. "Are you just going to let him go?"

There was sadness in Diane's eyes, but a gentle smile played on her lips. "Yes."

She didn't say anything else, so Faye turned to Wind again. "Isn't Diane your priority? You're just going to leave her?"

"I'm not leaving her. Diane's safe here, but Phoebe isn't. Shade needs my help. I'm sure he'd do the same for me if it'd been the other way around."

Shade grew tired of all of this. "Enough!" he yelled, making everyone in the room jump. "We're wasting time."

He grabbed the bag and headed for the door with irritated steps. The satchel was packed with food, clothing, and other things, like a flashlight, that might come in handy. Phoebe could be hurt, and here he was, watching Wind argue with Faye.

Arguing with Faye was pointless because she was stubborn. Telling her to shut up would only make her yell more. She just wouldn't listen, and he had no interest in remaining here one minute longer.

He jerked the front door open to storm out but came to a halt.

On the other side of the door stood a man Shade had never seen before.

The man was almost a head shorter than him. He was fit, with short, light brown hair that looked like it hadn't seen a comb for weeks, and judging by how the man smelled, he hadn't set a foot inside a shower for some time either.

He had a handsome face, but he was in desperate need of some cleaning up. His eyes were half-closed, as if he was tired, and he swayed from one foot to the other.

Shade's gaze narrowed. There was something wrong with the man.

The stranger eyed him from the bottom up. "Who are you?"

"Shade."

The man's voice was strange. It was slow, unclear, and just didn't sound normal.

Diane approached the door. "Scott? What the heck are you doing here?"

Scott ignored her and pushed himself through the front door.

Shade watched him enter the house.

Was he a friend of Phoebe's too?

Shade watched the man as a cat watched its prey. If he wasn't a friend, Shade would make the man regret interrupting him from trying to save Phoebe.

Shade gazed at Diane.

She didn't seem happy to see the man. Neither was Wind, Faye, or Celise.

Phoebe had a beautiful home, with wide and open spaces. Everything was in bright colors, making it appealing, but the man's presence spread an unnerving atmosphere.

The big hallway connected the living room on one side and the kitchen on the other.

Shade watched him disappear into the kitchen and come back a few seconds later.

"Where's the bitch?" Scott yelled as he ran from one room to the other, or tried to. He wavered around most of the time. It was a miracle he hadn't lost his balance yet.

Shade dropped the bag, and placed himself in Scott's way. Shade didn't even twitch a muscle when the man ran straight into him.

Scott groaned from the impact and fell to the floor.

No one came running to help him up.

Shade grabbed Scott's shirt and yanked him to his feet. "What bitch are you talking about?"

The man grabbed Shade's arms. "Let go of me, you big gorilla! Do you know who I am? I can have you arrested! If I don't find that little bitch soon, there will be hell to pay."

Shade raised an eyebrow. The man was obviously not afraid.

Wind approached, wearing his usually calm expression. "This is Scott, Shade. He's Phoebe's ex-boyfriend, and he's looking for Phoebe."

Shade's gaze jerked to Wind as agony surged through him. He remembered Phoebe talking on the phone with Faye a few weeks ago, mentioning someone named Scott, but he hadn't registered it at the time. He hadn't been fully functional then, but he was now. The pain of knowing that he was in front of a man Phoebe had slept with hurt like hell.

"I see what goes through your mind," Wind said, "but don't worry. Phoebe will never take him back. I promise you that. She's all yours."

Shade took a deep breath. He should know that. Phoebe was his, but she also had a history before him, and this man with his weird behavior was a part of it.

"He did nothing but hurt her when they were together. He mistreated her, constantly calling her names, and pushing her down."

Shade growled. "Does she still care for him?"

"No. If she'd been here, she would've told you to get him out of the house."

With a roar, Shade slammed Scott against the wall next to the front door.

Scott groaned and immediately stood straighter. He locked gazes with Shade and his eyes grew bigger as fear grabbed him.

Neither Diane, Wind, nor Celise, moved a muscle to stop Shade. Faye wasn't in the room. Where she'd gone didn't matter.

"You're a cyborg," Scott said with a gasp.

Shade snorted. "You notice that now?"

"He's drunk," Wind said.

"What does that mean?"

"I'll tell you later."

Shade returned his focus to Scott, pressing the man

harder against the wall. "You listen to me now, you little shit. I am Phoebe's, I am bound to her, meaning she is under my protection. You better leave and never come back. If I see your ugly face here again, I will turn your life into a living hell. Am I making myself clear?"

Disbelief filled Scott's face. "I can't believe she got herself a machine when she could've had a real man."

Shade's anger melted into rage. Phoebe was in danger, and here he was, arguing with an idiot. With another roar, Shade threw Scott out through the front door.

The man landed on his side on the ground, screaming as if something had broken.

Shade didn't care if Scott hurt himself. It wasn't his problem, but he couldn't leave him here while he and Wind were gone. That would only give Scott the chance to harass the women during their absence.

He grabbed the bag from the floor and turned to Wind. "Is there somewhere we can leave him?"

Wind nodded. "There is a police station where a few cyborgs work here in Glaswell. They will take care of him."

"Good. Where does he live?"

"On the other side of Glaswell, but if we tell the police what happened here today, they'll make sure he never comes back. He's been warned before."

"Even better." He slung the satchel over his shoulder. "We're leaving."

Wind turned to his bound one.

Diane put her thin arms around him. She tried to smile,

but her lips shook, and a tear ran down her cheek. "Come back to me." Her voice was low but loud enough for Shade to hear.

Shade glanced at Celise.

She stood silently next to Diane, with her lips pressed together. Celise wrung her hands and had her gaze fixed onto the floor. Not until Wind turned to her did she look up at him with huge eyes.

Wind grabbed her hands and gave her a gentle smile. "You did something amazing today, Celise. Thanks to you, we have a chance at saving Phoebe." He leaned forward.

When he kissed Celise on the cheek, she gasped. Her chin started to tremble, and tears pressed behind her eyes, but she managed to pull them back.

Shade frowned. Why did Wind kiss her? He belonged to Diane, and yet, he was intimate with another woman in front of his bound one, but judging by Diane's neutral expression, she didn't seem to mind.

Shade approached Celise. "Thank you. I appreciate all your help. If you ever need my help with something, don't be afraid to ask."

She gave him a shy smile. "I won't."

"Please contact Jade and tell her where we are going. We're going to need all the help we can get."

Celise nodded. "Of course. Diane and I will take care of that."

Diane looked around in the hallway. "Where did Faye go?"

Wind frowned. "I don't know. I didn't notice her leave. I was too focused on Shade and Scott."

"Me too," Celise said and looked down at the floor again.

"Maybe, she got angry at us for not being allowed to come along," Shade said.

"Yeah, she probably went home. She lives across the street," Diane said. "But that's just not like her, to give up on an argument."

Shade walked out the door and went straight for Scott. He grabbed his arm and pulled him to his feet.

Scott struggled against his grip. "You broke my arm, you bastard!"

"I'll break the other if you don't shut up."

He dragged Scott to the big white car in front of the house, opened the doors, and threw him inside.

Only one thing was on his mind — finding his bound one and kill anyone who'd hurt her.

CHAPTER 21

"She's in love with you," Shade told Wind as they drove along the country road.

Glaswell, and Scott, were far behind them. They'd left him at the police station, and the cyborg that worked there had promised to take care of the situation.

The further they came, the fewer trees there were. The green grass fields on both sides of the road slowly turned into sand and rocks, looking more and more like the wasteland they were heading for.

They'd been driving for almost two hours, and Shade had gotten used to being inside of a car. At first, the speed had bothered him. Wind had suggested slowing down, but that would only take them longer to reach Phoebe, so Shade sucked it up. At least, they weren't flying like he'd seen some cars do.

Wind frowned. "Who?"

"Celise."

He relaxed and smiled. "Oh. Yes, I know. She's been in love with me for years. I think everyone knows, but no one talks about it. Celise never says anything, either, but she's like an open book."

"What does that mean?"

"It means she's easy to read. Her heartbeat increases every time I come close. She breathes faster, and her body temperature rises. Celise avoids looking into my eyes, but I know she watches me when she thinks I don't see. Everything in her body language tells me she wants me."

Shade frowned. "I watched you before we left. You touched her. Why would you do that in front of your bound one? Why would you do that at all?"

"Because Diane told me to be kind to her. When Diane was younger, she was deeply in love with a man, and he knew it. Instead of being gentle, he ignored her. He treated her like she didn't exist. Diane told me it would've been more kind of him to turn her down with gentle words instead of showing her his back."

Shade nodded. "Diane doesn't want Celise to experience the same pain."

"Exactly. Besides, Celise is our friend, and her talents are amazing. She knows more about cyborgs than anyone I've ever encountered. Sometimes, I even think she knows more than Jade." Wind's lips twitched into a smile. "She comes by from time to time and examines me, making sure everything is working, that none of my programming or cybernetics are malfunctioning."

Shade blinked. "Why don't you turn her down? Celise should know that you will never be hers."

Wind's face tensed. "Celise knows."

"Have you spoken to her about it?"

Wind slowed the car and turned onto a smaller road. It seemed to be leading them straight out into the wastelands. Instead of trees, there were huge rocks.

They were getting closer to Phoebe. Shade felt it in his whole body.

"A few years ago," Wind answered, "but she never stopped loving me. She told me her heart just refuses to let me go."

Imagining what Celise went through wasn't difficult. Shade contemplated Phoebe turning him down, and pain instantly filled every part of his body. The difference between him and Celise was he'd die if Phoebe did that.

"And what do you think of it all?" Shade asked.

Wind appeared to think for a while. "I like her. She's kind and intelligent, but as you said, she and I can never be. As a bound cyborg, I'm not capable of evolving such feelings for anyone else but my bound one."

"One day, you will have to talk to her about it again. You can't let it go on. It hurts her and will, sooner or later, affect your friendship."

He snorted. "You know, for being a newborn cyborg, you know a lot about life."

"I learn fast. Besides, it's not that hard to imagine what she's going through."

Wind took a deep breath. "No, it's not." He placed his hand on his chest while he held the steering wheel with the other. "I feel the bond every minute of the day. My thoughts are always on Diane. Whenever I'm away from her, I miss her. It hurts to be apart from her."

Shade couldn't have agreed more. He was nothing without his Phoebe. She was the reason he was breathing.

If the Fighters did anything to her ...

He shook his head. He didn't want to think about it. Not when they were so close. They needed to change the subject. This ride would become too long otherwise.

"Explain to me what drunk means," he barked.

The cyborg gave him a quick glance before he turned his focus back onto the road. "Do you know what alcohol is?"

"No." He couldn't recall ever hearing anything about 'alcohol' during his month at MedAct.

The Internet hadn't interested him enough yet to find out more about the world that way. Shade had touched it with his mind a few times, but all the chaos online always overwhelmed him.

"It's something the humans drink. It can be turned into many different beverages, like beer, vodka, liqueur, and so on. Each drink tastes different, but they all have the same effect on the body."

"What effect?"

"You saw it on Scott's behavior. It can literally turn a person into a rambling idiot who's unaware of what they're doing. And if you drink too much, you might even wake up the following day with no memory of what you've done. And on top of that, you'll have a major headache."

Shade stared at Wind. He had a hard time believing

what he was hearing.

"Alcohol can't affect us, but the humans often react to it in bad ways. I've seen it a few times and I don't recommend it. Thankfully, most humans drink in moderation."

He frowned. "Why drink at all?"

Wind shrugged. "You tell me. Most of it doesn't even smell nice, but you have nothing to worry about. One of the demands placed on the humans that sign up for a cyborg is that they don't drink alcohol. Another is that they don't smoke. MedAct has a long list of things that the humans can't do, ever, if they want to apply for a cyborg."

Shade frowned. "Smoke?"

Wind grinned. "I'll explain another time." He slowed down the car and turned onto a narrow, unpaved road. "We're almost there."

He looked out through the window. Wasteland surrounded them. A few dried trees were strewn on each side of the road. The beige and brown ground was filled with sand and rocks instead of healthy grass.

Neither he, nor Wind, knew what awaited them, but they knew they'd arrive at a house in the middle of nowhere. Nothing but sand would surround the house.

That was what Celise had told them. That also meant there was no way of surprising the Fighters who were inside it. Besides, they were probably expected.

Shade wouldn't be surprised if they knew that someone had messed with the signal that linked all cyborgs. Things like that weren't a secret from cyborgs for long, especially when all cyborgs felt it at the same time.

"Did you hear that?" Wind frowned.

"Hear what?"

"Something is moving inside the car."

He focused and tried to pick up what Wind had heard. At first, he didn't hear anything but the engine and the wheels rolling along the road.

But then it came. A loud thud from behind, probably the trunk.

They looked at it each other.

"What was that?" Shade asked.

"I have no idea, but we better find out."

Wind slowed and parked the car along the side of the road. There were no cars passing in either direction. The chance of them encountering another car had become scarcer with each mile they'd put behind them. It'd already been over ten minutes since they'd last seen a car.

They exited the car and approached the trunk.

Wind's face bore a serious expression.

Shade had a bad feeling about this.

Wind put his hand against the trunk and closed his eyes. "Please, let it not be who I think it is." He opened the trunk.

First, Shade saw a leg, then a T-shirt before he looked higher and stared right into Faye's blue eyes.

Wind sighed. "Why am I not surprised?"

Faye sat up and gave them a grin. "It was about time you opened the trunk. Do you know you can't open it from the inside? I sure do now." She reached out to Wind. "Help me

155

out, will you?"

He didn't move right away. Anger flashed in his eyes. He grabbed Faye's arm and yanked her out of the car. "What do you think you're doing?"

Faye fixed her clothes. "I'm going with you. I told you that." She pulled her long, blonde hair from her golden ponytail holder and started to put it up again.

"I knew you were stubborn," Wind said, "but I never expected you to be stupid."

She glared at him. "I'm not stupid for trying to help my friend. You boys are going to need me, whether you're aware of it or not."

"What are you talking about?"

"Remember Silver? He'll be there. You two did a good job pissing him off. He might listen to me."

"What makes you so sure?" Shade asked. "The last time you two met was more like he was making fun of you."

She shrugged. "I just have a feeling, and I always listen to my feelings. You'd be surprised how much they can tell you, so suck it up, boys. I'm not going anywhere."

CHAPTER 22

The house was bigger than Shade had expected. It wasn't really a house either, not anymore at least. There was only one floor, but a part of the roof had collapsed and had brought down the walls in the process. Most of the windows had bars, and a terrace of old and worn-out wooden panels was in front of the front door. The house had been beautifully painted in yellow once. Now, only paint flakes decorated the walls.

Shade looked around. The house was the only one standing, but here and there, there were ruins of other homes. Everything was surrounded by dull and lifeless wasteland. In the far distance, there were majestic mountains, and the sun was slowly disappearing behind them.

"I don't like this," Faye said from the backseat.

"Me neither," Wind said.

Shade kept scanning the surroundings. "What is this place?"

"This used to be a flourishing town about a hundred years ago, long before there were any cyborgs in the world," Wind answered. "The ground started dying and people moved away, leaving the town to its fate. This is what remains of it."

"A perfect hideout for the Fighters," Shade said.

"I doubt this is their main hideout. This place is too easy to find."

"We should try another approach," Faye said.

Wind stopped the car a short distance away from the house, and irritation crossed his features as he turned to Faye. "You shouldn't be here in the first place, so you *will* stay in the car."

Her chin dropped. "No way!"

"Don't argue with me, Faye. You've already done enough. You should be glad we'd come this far before we discovered you. Otherwise, I would've turned back to make sure you stayed with Diane and Celise, where you would have been safe." He took a breath to calm himself. "The Fighters are dangerous. I have no idea what they're planning, but I'll do my best to protect you. And if protecting you means you staying in the car, then that's what you're going to do. Do you understand?"

Faye glared at him but didn't say anything.

Shade had no interest in joining the argument. They'd spoken of little else since they'd discovered Faye in the trunk.

The irritation in the car felt like a thick wall, and Wind, who was usually composed, looked like he'd snap any second if Faye kept arguing with him.

She believed she could reach Silver, make him think things through, and change his mind, but Nightmare was the Fighter's leader, not Silver.

Shade had no idea what kind of rankings the cyborg had among the Fighters, but in the end, it was Nightmare's words that counted.

That much he understood about the Fighters after reading up on them on the Internet during his time at MedAct.

They followed their leader.

Overall, there wasn't much inside information, but the Fighters had been caught on camera plenty of times, revealing a pattern.

They robbed places for provisions, and they killed anyone who stood in their way.

They rarely hurt innocent people, but police officers or MedAct's soldier cyborgs were killed without a second thought.

Luckily for MedAct, they could repair most of their cyborgs, but the police officers were human and didn't stand a chance against the Fighters.

Why a human would stand in a Fighter's way in the first place was beyond him. They should know their efforts were pointless, and yet, they tried to take down the rogue cyborgs over and over again.

Why the police stations sent out human officers to the crime scenes was another mystery.

Sometimes, Shade just couldn't understand how humans thought. After watching plenty of videos from the surveillance cameras, he got the feeling that some thought they were invincible.

Despite the Fighters, the humans didn't seem to mind having cyborgs around, according to what he'd found out, and that pleased him.

MedAct had proven a long time ago that they knew what they were doing, and people decided to trust that, and over the years, they'd gotten used to the cyborgs.

Male cyborgs were now a part of the society, but there were no female cyborgs. He didn't know why. He had no information about it, and there had been none to find, either.

But there were some who despised cyborgs. Shade had read articles about people trying to attack cyborgs or trying to take down MedAct. Of course, those missions had failed, and such situations were rare. Those humans must've had something wrong with their heads.

Humans didn't have any programming or cybernetics as he and the other cyborgs did, but some of them seemed to need an update.

Their irrational actions were difficult to understand. Shade still had a lot to learn as a newborn cyborg, but even he understood the consequences of what would happen if he attacked someone who was stronger than him. Some humans seemed to lack that logic, though.

A sound from the house brought his attention back to the present.

Faye and Wind looked up, too.

It had been the door. The old wood and the rusty hinges

squeaked as the door opened.

Four Fighters left the house. Nightmare was in the lead, with Silver right behind him. The other two followed.

Silver wore a dark grin of excitement, but Nightmare appeared emotionless. His eyes were as cold as ice. His determined expression revealed a hint of danger if any of them dared to confront him the wrong way.

Nightmare was the most ruthless and the most dangerous Fighter of all the Fighters. Shade had learned that from reading the Internet. Nightmare never doubted, he never thought twice and would do anything in his power to survive.

MedAct, and the people there, had once been his home.

Now, they were his enemy.

Without taking his eyes off of Nightmare, Shade opened the car door and got out.

Wind followed.

Faye, to his surprise, remained seated, but she held the car door slightly open.

They walked a few steps forward, putting themselves in front of the car.

Shade assessed the situation.

The Fighters behind Silver looked unpredictable. He had no idea what they would do or what they were capable of, but he suspected they'd do anything Nightmare told them to do.

The one to the right was tall and muscular with androgynous features and blond hair.

Shade had never seen such emotionless eyes before. Nightmare's eyes were cold, but this cyborg showed nothing.

Nothing at all.

The other one was shorter, slimmer, but with masculine features and light brown hair. He didn't look as strong as the other Fighters, but Shade suspected he was fast and could pull off a deadly attack with the dagger that hung by his hip.

"I must say, I didn't expect you to show up so fast, and you brought your friends," Nightmare said. "I thought it would take you longer to find us, but I guess that buzzing in our heads told you where we were."

Shade's gaze narrowed. Of course, they knew about the signal. They'd figured it out faster than he'd expected, but at the same time, it didn't surprise him. They were cyborgs after all.

"At first, we thought MedAct was up to something, but once Heaven," he nodded toward the blond Fighter, "confirmed it wasn't them, I realized it had to be you, or someone from your surroundings." Nightmare took a step closer. "Tell me, how did you do it?"

Shade ignored his question. "Where is Phoebe?"

Nightmare's gaze darkened and a tiny grin appeared on his lips, but it disappeared fast. "She's safe. We don't hurt humans unless we have to."

That much he'd figured out. "Let her go."

Nightmare snorted. "Do you really think we went through all of that trouble just to let her go?"

Shade didn't care. "I want to see her."

"Sure. All you have to do is follow me inside the house."

Warning bells rang inside his head. Entering the house was the last thing he should do, but Phoebe was in there. He could feel that she was near. He shot Wind a glance.

Wind's lips tensed, but he gave him a nod.

He turned to Nightmare. "I'll go with you."

"Not enough," Nightmare growled. "All of you are coming with us, even the woman in the car."

Shade winced. "It's me you want, isn't it?

"Yes."

"Then I'm the only one going."

The Fighter's leader opened his mouth to say something, but the door to the car flung open.

Faye slammed the door shut and approached them.

Wind sighed and Shade didn't miss the wide grin on Silver's face.

"I told you to stay in the car," Wind said.

"And he said," she pointed at Nightmare, "that we all must go inside the house if we want Phoebe back." There was no fear in her expression, but there was an underlying insecurity in her self-assured posture. She looked the Fighters right in the eyes.

For that, Shade admired her. She was a small human female, weaker than most human males, and here she was, standing up against the unreliable Fighters.

"Are we going, or not?" Faye asked.

Shade and Wind had no choice but to follow her. Any unexpected move and the Fighters might attack, so grabbing

Faye to push her back was out of the question. She wouldn't agree and would make a scene that they didn't need right now.

She stopped in front of Nightmare and crossed her arms over her chest, giving him an angry glare. "I assume you're Nightmare. You look like him from all the images I've seen."

He tilted his head slightly, taking in Faye slowly with a gaze that didn't show much interest. "And you are?"

"Faye Summers. I'm a friend of Phoebe's and if you have so much as pulled out a hair from her head, you'll have to deal with me."

Nightmare raised an eyebrow before his gaze darted to Shade and Wind. "A brave one." He looked at Faye again. He towered over her with his tall frame and broad shoulders. He was at least twice the size of her. "Tell me, little one." He leaned forward, maybe expecting Faye to flinch away, but she didn't move an inch. "What exactly can a little female like you do to hurt me?"

"More than you can image," she hissed through her teeth.

His lips twitched and amusement sparked in his eyes. "I'm all ears."

She snorted. "Do you really think I'll give away my secrets? Please, don't take me for a fool, but I can assure you you're making a mistake if you judge me by my size."

Nightmare's amusement died and Shade had no other option but to silence Faye. He grabbed her arm and pulled her against him. "Shut up, Faye. You're making things worse."

Faye tore herself free from his grip.

Silver laughed and took a step closer. "Feisty, little female, isn't she?" He reached toward her face but didn't touch her.

Faye didn't move.

"How about you and I find that room we never got the chance to visit?" he grinned.

Faye gave Silver a once-over and blushed.

Shade frowned. She had no issues playing strong and fearless in front of Nightmare, but when Silver came closer, she became a shy schoolgirl who was talking to her crush for the first time.

Shade cringed on the inside. The last thing they needed was Faye becoming interested in one of the Fighters. It would only end badly.

"Dream on, big boy. You're not getting anything from me."

Silver's grin widened. "We'll see about that." He looked at Nightmare. "She's mine." When he turned back at Faye, he licked his lips and desire radiated from his gaze. "All mine."

Chapter 23

Phoebe walked around the metal cage Nightmare had put her in several hours ago. A chair stood inside it, with a small table next to it. On it stood a plate with the remains of her dinner and a glass of water. At least, they fed her. No one had hurt her, and any Fighter who tried to get closer to her had to deal with Nightmare.

He'd commanded that the Fighters leave her be. She had no idea why he defended her from the others, but she was grateful, even if she didn't say it.

The living room and the kitchen were one big room connected with the hallway that led to several bedrooms and the front door. The cage stood in the middle of it all. There were plenty of windows in the living room, and they were protected by bars, making her wonder what this house had once been.

There were no curtains stopping the strong sunlight from entering, but at least, it didn't give her a headache. Sand was all over the floor; the walls were a dull yellowish color. Everything looked old. Even the air smelled old, but she doubted this was where the Fighters usually resided.

For one, there were too few Fighters here. She'd seen eight in total and there were a lot more out there. Secondly, this place was a mess. Whoever wanted to live like this?

A Fighter leaned against the wall. His shining eyes were set on her, but he didn't speak. His gaze was intense, but his body looked tired, marked by a hard life. His black hair hung down his shoulders in tangles, and he needed new clothes.

The black t-shirt and blue jeans he wore had seen better days. He hadn't said a single word to her, but she'd heard Nightmare and Silver address him. His name was Hunter, and he looked just as dangerous as the others. Fortunately, he lacked that mad look in his eyes that some of them had.

Fear had lingered in her mind ever since her conversation with Nightmare. She hadn't liked him touching her, but he hadn't done anything to her, just leaning against her, searching for nearness to another being. His actions had not been the reason for her fear, though.

His words had been.

Nightmare believed he could remove Shade's bond to her without killing him. Nightmare hadn't explained, but it'd broken her heart in two.

She'd cried her eyes out, begging him not to do it, but he hadn't moved a muscle. Instead, he told her someone had to be the first.

Phoebe had no idea what awaited now, but the stress made her stomach turn. The pain in her chest refused to go away. All she could think of was Shade, praying he'd stay away.

There was a gurney in the living room. It was wide, big enough for a cyborg. Next to it stood some kind of machine. It was slim and had a metallic aluminum color. On the top was a black screen with no buttons. Cords were attached as well. They hung down the side of it.

It all sent a cold chill through her, and this was the place where Nightmare planned to remove Shade's bond to her, with that awful machine. It didn't look painless. Instead, it reminded her more and more of a horror movie.

At least, there was no blood ... yet.

She closed her eyes when the thought of Shade on that gurney hit her. She could almost hear him scream and see him wriggle to get free.

There was a sound outside of an approaching car. Her fear magnified. It could only mean one thing ... "No," she gasped.

Hunter looked outside. Nightmare, Silver, and two other Fighters came rushing into the room and peered through the window.

Silver grinned. "It's time."

Nightmare opened the front door and left the house with Silver and the other two Fighters.

One of them was handsome with blond hair and emotionless eyes.

She'd heard the other's call him Heaven, but judging by his dead expression, he had little to do with anything that came close to heaven.

Silence filled the house. Phoebe had no idea what went

on outside, but all Fighters remaining inside gathered in the living room. They were all tall, muscular, and dangerous. No one smiled, said a word, or looked at her. They seemed to be preparing themselves.

Restlessness made her want to crawl out of her own skin. She couldn't stand still and biting her nails didn't ease her pain. Even if she couldn't see outside, she knew Shade had arrived.

Every minute Nightmare and the other Fighters were gone felt like an eternity.

"Run," she whispered even if Shade couldn't hear her. "Please, please ..." She grabbed the cage bars, her gaze fixed on the front door. After a while, she heard footsteps approach the house. The tension inside of her grew as Nightmare enter the house, followed by his Fighters and ... Shade. "Shade!"

His gaze instantly locked onto her. He pushed himself through the Fighters and ran to her. Metal bars were between them, but he didn't seem to care, and neither did she.

Phoebe wrapped her arms around him the best she could and pressed her lips to his.

Shade answered to her plea, kissing her back frantically.

"You shouldn't have come here," she said with mixed feelings of pure happiness and despair.

"I had to," Shade said.

Phoebe noticed movement in front of her and looked up. Her gaze landed on two familiar faces. "Wind? Faye?"

She didn't get the chance to say anything else.

Nightmare pulled out a gun and pointed it at Wind.

Wind tensed but didn't move.

Faye's jaw dropped and her eyes widened, but she remained silent.

"We don't have much time, so let's get started, shall we?" Nightmare said. "Hunter, open the cage."

The black-haired Fighter approached, pulled out a key from his pocket, and opened the door.

"Get inside, all of you," Nightmare said.

"You're going to regret this," Shade barked, but he didn't disobey.

Nightmare was probably not the only one with a gun, and even if the others didn't have guns, he still had seven Fighters on his side who didn't care if they lived or died.

"You think I'm the dangerous one?" Nightmare snorted and shrugged. "Well, I guess I am most of the time, but you don't want to mess with Heaven." He nodded toward the blond Fighter. His face was emotionless, his gaze set on them. "He's the one without emotions. It's all logic with him. When his bound one died a few years ago, he almost died with her, making him turn off his emotions in the process, so if there's anyone to fear, it's him." His gaze darkened as he grinned and handed over the gun to Heaven.

The blond Fighter's expressionless face didn't change as he pointed the gun at Wind. His eyes were cold, dead, almost as if he lacked a soul. An unpleasant atmosphere surrounded him, an atmosphere of emptiness. "Move," Heaven said with an almost robotic voice.

Wind looked tense, but he did as Heaven said.

He and Faye entered the cage.

Phoebe hugged them all and Hunter locked the door behind them.

Thankfully, there was enough room for them all to stand, but barely enough space to move around.

Wind gave her a gentle smile as he hugged her, and Faye's hug was, as always, intense and strong.

"I'm so glad to see you," she said with a smile and gave them a thankful gaze. "But you shouldn't have come." She looked at Shade. "They're after you." She put her arms around him, and tears stuck in her throat. "I know what they want to do."

Shade gently caressed her hair. "What?"

"Nightmare believes he can remove the bond without killing you."

CHAPTER 24

Pain surged through Shade when he heard Phoebe's words.

Nightmare wanted to part them.

He wanted to take Phoebe away from him, to turn him into one of the Fighters.

Anger followed when agony faded, but Shade refused to give Nightmare the pleasure of seeing his reaction. The bastard was watching them intently.

Shade wrapped his arms tighter around Phoebe. No one would take her away from him. Anyone who tried would pay with their life, and Nightmare was one Fighter the world wouldn't miss.

"Your bound one speaks the truth," the Fighter's leader said.

The cyborg who Nightmare had called Hunter, stood guard by the cage next to Heaven. Their faces looked as if they were carved out of stone, and their gazes rested on everyone inside the cage.

Heaven still held the gun, but he didn't aim it at anyone any longer.

Silver joined them, but his expression was different.

He was grinning. He seemed filled with anticipation, just waiting for something to happen.

There were also some Fighters by the windows and the door. The other Fighter who'd been outside with Heaven and Nightmare stopped by the machine near the gurney. He pressed the screen. The machine came on.

"You better start talking. Why are you doing this?" Shade growled at Nightmare.

His lips twitched. "Sure, we have some time to kill while Edge prepares everything." He walked around the room with his hand against his chin. "How shall I put it?" He turned toward the cage and looked Shade in the eyes. "You've all been screwed."

"What do you mean?" He narrowed his gaze.

Nightmare glanced at Phoebe. "How much did you learn about the history of cyborgs while you went to MedAct's school?"

"Just the basics," she said.

Nightmare raised his hand, gesturing for her to go on. "Tell me."

Phoebe tensed. It was obvious; the last thing she wanted was to talk to Nightmare. "It wasn't really anything new. Most people know the story. Cyborgs were created by Doctor Carolyn Williams and her team about fifty years ago. They were also the ones behind MedAct. In the beginning, MedAct was only a medical company, creating drugs and cures for the people, but somehow, they stumbled onto technology and cybernetics, developing all kinds of technologies. It was everything from machines that took care of household matters to advanced computers. MedAct also worked with the human body on a cellular level, I recall reading. They created human organs that could be exchanged or grown directly inside the body."

"Go on," Nightmare said when Phoebe became silent.

She sighed. "Fine. Don't ask me how, but somehow, they came up with the idea for cyborgs, but the cyborgs couldn't live. No one knew why, until Doctor Carolyn Williams decided to bind one to herself. She discovered there was a malfunction in their programming, and by binding a cyborg to herself, she could keep him steady and alive. That's how the bond came to be."

"Yes, that's the official story," Nightmare said, "but most of it is bullshit." He turned to Wind and Shade. "That's the information you had about MedAct when you woke up, isn't it? They gave you everything they wanted you to believe and you didn't question it one bit."

"You're mad," Wind hissed between his teeth. "Why should we trust anything you say?"

Anger flashed in his dark eyes. "Because *I* was the cyborg Carolyn bound to herself!"

Silence filled the room.

Shade stood stunned, just staring at him.

Nightmare finally took a deep breath, as to calm himself. "I was fine ... and very much alive ... long before she bound me to her. There never was any need for a bond for us to live."

Doubt grew inside Shade. Trusting Nightmare was the last thing he'd ever do, but he needed to hear what the cyborg had to say. "So why did she bind you to her?"

"There were four of us. From the moment we opened our eyes the doctors and scientists treated us like brainless machines. They didn't care that we had feelings, and apart from our cybernetics, we were human," Nightmare said. "After a few years, we became tired of being lab rats and revolted. It didn't go well. The others lost their lives. I got hurt but survived. Carolyn wasn't happy with our actions and decided to try her latest experiment on me. The bond." He spit out the word like a curse. "She bound me to her to make sure a revolt would never happen again. And it worked. Carolyn forced me to fall in love with the woman I hated the most in the entire world. Do you have any idea what it's like to feel love and hate at the same time for the person you are bound to? Or what it's like to have intercourse with that person?" Nightmare's eyes sparked with anger. "My body desired her, but my mind despised her. Things like that can drive you crazy, and I lived like that for several years."

A small part of Shade felt sorry for the cyborg. He had a hard time believing him, but it was obvious he'd been through a lot. The question was; what if what Nightmare said was true? There was no doubt in Shade's mind that Nightmare believed everything he said. "How did Carolyn Williams die?"

Nightmare snorted. "I didn't kill her, if that's what you're asking, but believe me, I wanted to. I just couldn't do it, because of the bond. And I am aware of the rumors that my bound one was murdered, but they are all false. No, Carolyn had an easy way out. She was killed by a drunk driver, and that was the end." He shrugged. "Just like that, I was free from the bond, but not the pain."

"Why did you hate her?" Faye asked.

"Weren't you listening to what I just said? Because she didn't give a shit about me. I was nothing more but an experiment to her, and once she found a way to control us, she made sure to use it in every newborn cyborg after that. I watched it happen in front of my eyes. Newborn cyborgs who didn't know better. They were in love with their bound ones from the moment they opened their eyes, and they never questioned it because they were happy." He shook his head. "If only they'd known how their love had come to be. Fear has always been a means for control among humans, but Carolyn discovered love was a stronger force. She convinced every scientist and doctor that cyborgs can't live without the bond, that the other three had died because they weren't bound, and I guess the rest is history."

Faye snorted. "I guess you blame everyone at MedAct for what was done to you."

He shot her a glare that said: "*be careful*". "MedAct is the enemy, and they must go down. The doctor who created you," he looked at Shade and Wind, "Jade Silva, she has taken over Carolyn's work. She will be the first to die as soon as I get my hands on her."

"You will not touch Jade," Shade growled. He didn't like

her much, but Jade was not the enemy. "Carolyn Williams died about forty years ago. Jade wasn't even born then. You have no idea what she's done with Carolyn's work."

"Jade makes sure the bond is there, doesn't she? That's enough for me. Jade knows cyborgs can exist without the bond. It was all written in Carolyn's papers."

Shade shook his head. "You really are crazy."

Nightmare's expression remained stern. "Believe what you want. Soon, you'll see things from a different perspective." He turned toward the cyborg who stood by the machine. He was still pressing buttons, probably putting in a program. "How is it going, Edge?"

Edge didn't look up. "A few more minutes."

Nightmare nodded and paced the living room.

"Why me?" Shade asked.

Nightmare's gaze shot back to Shade. "Because you're newborn. I've had my eyes on MedAct for years. It's not difficult to get access to their projects and find what I'm looking for. I'm the oldest cyborg out there after all, aren't I?"

"That was how you knew about me," Shade snarled.

"Yes, and that's why I sent Silver there. He allowed himself to get caught by MedAct and play their little game of finding a new bound one for him. It didn't really go as planned, but it went a lot better. You came straight to him for a little chit-chat. It gave him the chance to scan you, to see if you were the right one for this experiment."

"And you were," Silver grinned. "I knew they'd eventually

want to transfer me to a place they say other unbound cyborgs live, and that would be my way out. It was perfectly timed with your sign-out from MedAct, thanks to us. Getting into their system is way too easy."

"What is that place they wanted to ship you to?" Faye asked.

Silver shrugged and moved closer to the cage where she stood. "I have no idea, sweetheart. No cyborg is given information about that place. We don't even know what it's called, but MedAct gladly keeps telling us we will be shipped somewhere if we don't agree to bind ourselves to a new person. We haven't been able to find any information about it, either. Strange, don't you think?" He winked and his gaze traveled hungrily down the length of her body. "But you made me almost consider binding myself. You're hot and feisty enough to make me want to tame you."

Faye grinned. She grabbed the bars and glared into his eyes with determination. "Oh, really?" She looked him over the way he'd looked her over, then snorted as if she wasn't pleased with what she saw. "A guy like you would never be able to keep up with me."

Irritation flashed in his eyes. "Want to find out?"

Phoebe grabbed Faye and pulled her away from the bars with a wary look in her eyes. "Whatever you do, don't touch him in an intimate way."

Faye frowned. "Why not?"

"An unbound cyborg can't touch a woman that doesn't have a bound one. If Silver touches you intimately, the bonding process will initiate. Even a little kiss is enough, so quit your teasing, and stay away from him."

Faye stared at Phoebe, aghast.

Shade was shocked himself. That was new information to him, and Wind seemed just as surprised.

"Who told you that?" Wind asked.

Phoebe looked at the Fighters leader. "He did."

Faye stood mute for several minutes. Her gaze eventually turned to Silver.

He gave her a grin. "Still interested?"

She straightened her back. "The last thing I want is a buffoon like you bound to me." She nodded toward Nightmare. "I'd rather take him than you."

The Fighter lunged at the cage, trying to grab Faye, but Shade and Wind pulled her behind them.

Something wasn't right with the Fighter's mind.

After all, none of the Fighters seemed sane.

Nightmare was a complete madman if he believed in the fairytale he'd told them, and Silver played a dangerous game. He wanted to remain free, but if he touched a woman, he'd bind himself to her. Playing with Faye was playing with fire.

Heaven hadn't moved a muscle. He just watched them with his emotionless eyes, waiting for an order. It was almost as if he would remain in that same spot for eternity if Nightmare didn't tell him to do something else.

Edge, who still stood by the machine, seemed to be a little ... well, edgy. His head jerked from one side to the other from time to time, as if he had muscle spasms. He shifted his weight from one foot to the other several times per minute, almost as if he had too much energy and didn't know what to do with it.

The other Fighters in the living room didn't look much better.

Neither Shade nor Wind said anything to Silver. They just glared at him, warning him that if he tried anything, he would lose a finger or more.

Nightmare looked bored. "Give it a rest, Silver. You don't want the little female to trigger the wrong sides of you." He turned to Edge. "Time?"

"Two minutes."

"Good." He came closer to the cage, pushing Silver away in the process. "Here's the thing." He looked at Shade. "You can either co-operate with us or we'll tie you down. It won't be pretty if we have to do that, and I don't think you want your dear Phoebe to see us hurting you."

Shade looked at Phoebe.

There were traces of tears in her eyes. She wasn't crying now, but the thought that someone had hurt her during his absence filled him with rage. He felt like a ticking time bomb, ready to go off at any second if the Fighters touched her.

He would do anything for her. His love for her lingered inside his body as if it were his life force. She was his breath, his life, his everything ... and he would die for her.

He turned to Nightmare. "Let them go, and I'll do what you want."

CHAPTER 25

Phoebe gasped. "No! I won't let you." She grabbed Shade's arm in a desperate attempt to make him see reason.

There was so much love in his beautiful, shiny eyes, it almost tore her apart. He didn't want to do it. He didn't want to break their bond, but they were surrounded by cyborgs. Getting out of here in one piece seemed almost like an impossible task.

"I don't want to lose you." Her chin trembled.

"You really do love him, don't you?" Nightmare asked.

Phoebe turned an angry glare on him. "Yes, and I'd bet you have no idea what love is. You're nothing but a monster."

His gaze darkened. "Do you think I'm doing this to hurt you or Shade? I've been working on this for years, and I can assure you it will be painless for him."

"If it works," she said.

Nightmare remained silent for a while. "It will work."

"And then what?"

"And then, he'll be the first cyborg free to follow what his heart tells him without MedAct's interference." He threw out his arms. "Look at us. We all have been marked from losing our bound ones. Shade will not experience that. He'll be free. If he still wants to be with you once the bond is gone, then so be it. I'm not an impossible cyborg. All I want is to find a way out of the bond. Then, I'll be able to free all cyborgs from the lie the bond is."

"What about the cyborgs who don't want to be free from the bond? Have you thought about that, or are you going to force them like you're forcing Shade now?"

"The bond is not real!" Nightmare roared, making Phoebe jump back.

"It's real to me," Wind said with a cold voice. "I will kill you if you try to remove my bond to my bound one."

Nightmare snorted. "Once Shade is free, it will be your turn whether you like it or not. If it works for him, it will work for an older cyborg, but I will not try to set an older cyborg free before I'm sure it works for a newborn. Everything is new to Shade and so is the bond. Your bond is set like a rock inside of you."

"Do you honestly think my bond isn't set just because I'm newborn?" Disbelief filled Shade's voice.

"I know it's not. As I said, I've spent years studying this. I know what I'm doing. Besides, you all walked in here freely, so don't blame me for being in this situation."

"We would not have *been* in this situation if you hadn't taken Phoebe."

Nightmare shrugged. "I wasn't able to snatch you from MedAct, so I had to make sure you'd come to me, and since you're a cyborg, I knew it wouldn't take long for you to figure out where I was … if I stayed in sight." Nightmare shifted his weight to his other foot. "But I'm still curious as to how you found that signal." He looked them over. "You taught me something important today. I never believed the signal could be used for tracking. If MedAct knew about this …" He shook his head and took a deep breath. "But I guess it's just a matter of time before they find out."

"It's done." Edge straightened his back, looking at Nightmare.

Nightmare nodded and glanced at Shade. "So how will it be?"

Phoebe put her arms around Shade, holding him hard to try to stop him. Her heart was being ripped apart. She was losing him. It made her want to scream with despair.

"As I said, let them go, and I will do it."

Nightmare shrugged. "Deal."

"Please, don't do it. Stay with me. I love you," she whispered. With every word, her voice shook more.

Shade cupped her face between his strong hands and made her look up. It was almost impossible to hold back her tears as she watched his handsome but determined face.

He was her everything. Her reason for living. She wouldn't be able to go on without him. It would destroy her.

"You'll never lose me, no matter what happens. I promise you."

He pressed his lips to hers and Phoebe felt his heat and desire surround her.

She gave in to his demanding kiss, allowing him access

to her mouth. He made promises with his tongue as he swept it against hers. It told her that he'd never abandon her, that his heart would always belong to her.

Hunter approach the cage. He put the key in the lock and opened the door.

"Hurry up," Nightmare said to Shade, with no respect whatsoever for her situation. It was all about him, his Fighters, and his quest to end the bond.

Shade pressed her against him in a strong embrace. "I love you," he whispered in her ear. "Don't ever question that."

"I won't," she sobbed, finally unable to stop the tears from coming. Phoebe let them run down her cheeks. It didn't take long before her eyes became warm and sensitive from the swelling that followed. Whatever happened now, she'd fight for him.

She would never abandon him.

He was her life and she needed him. She needed him more than the air she breathed. She wouldn't let Nightmare destroy them. Shade's love for her was real. It wasn't *just* the bond.

It was a lot more.

They already had a history together, and that meant something too. Shade *would* remember that. He *would* remember and come back to her. He'd remember her love for him.

Phoebe could do nothing but watch as he stepped out from the cage.

Fighters approached him with a purpose in their eyes. One hasty move from Shade and they'd jump him.

Silver grinned. "I must admit, you're a brave one. I would've resisted until my last breath."

There was no amusement in Shade's face. "That's why you're the stupid one. Do you really think I'll risk Phoebe's life, or my friends' lives? I'm fully aware of what will happen if I don't agree to this."

Faye approaching the open cage door, but Phoebe didn't care why. Her emotions were all over the place, and she was unable to pull herself together.

Wind stood behind her with his hands on her shoulders. He was trying to give her support, but it didn't help much.

Nightmare stopped in front of Shade. "Defending your bound one, aren't you?" He snorted. "I wouldn't put too much faith into her love. After all, she didn't stop me from being intimate with her. It was way too easy."

Ice shot down Phoebe's spine and into her chest.

It was as if the air in the house suddenly solidified when Shade tensed. The rage in his eyes sent another frigid shudder all over her. Her heart raced as her palms became perspired. She had to explain to Shade that nothing had happened, that Nightmare hadn't given her a choice. He needed to know the truth ...

Phoebe grabbed the bars. "No, it's ..."

Shade clenched his fists. His words to Silver forgotten as he struck Nightmare in the face.

The Fighter jerked sideways from the blow. He groaned,

pain contorting his features.

Shade roared and prepared another strike, but Edge, Hunter, and a third unknown Fighter jumped him.

Phoebe screamed. Fear shook the deepest parts of her soul as she watched them force Shade to the floor.

He fought them, struggling against their grips. He managed to hit Edge but got hit back. Shade grunted.

Someone cursed and Shade roared again as other hands made sure he stayed put.

"Stop it!" Phoebe yelled, lunging for the cage's exit, but hands grabbed her from behind. She turned around and saw Wind.

"Don't," he said. "They will hurt you."

She wiggled in his arms. "Let go of me! I have to help him."

Wind didn't obey. Instead, he pulled her away from the exit, where Faye stood as if paralyzed.

Faye's eyes were filled with terror as she watched the scene.

Nightmare straightened and massaged his cheek. "Sedate him," he growled.

Phoebe struggled in Wind's arms. "Don't touch him, you monsters!"

The cyborgs didn't listen. They didn't care. To them, she was invisible.

Silver moved closer to the cage's exit with his gaze set on Shade, who wrestled with Edge and Hunter on the floor. He held a syringe.

She wouldn't let him get near Shade with that thing. "I swear to God if you touch him with it, I'll poke it in your eye!"

Silver placed himself just a few feet from Faye, but he looked straight at Phoebe, with rage in his shining eyes. "That's a brave threat, woman."

Phoebe glared. A hatred she'd never felt in her entire life filled her. She'd make them all pay for treating her, Shade, and her friends like this. They *would* regret it. Somehow, she'd make sure of it.

She opened her mouth to make sure Silver understood that, but before a single word had the chance to leave her mouth, Faye lunged at Silver.

His eyes widened when Faye grabbed his face and pressed her lips to his. He jerked, tried to pull away ... and then, he stilled.

Silence filled the room.

Everyone stared at Silver and Faye.

The syringe fell to the floor.

CHAPTER 26

It was as if time itself had stopped, as if the air had left the room, turning every face pale. The silence was so deafening it almost hurt, and it seemed to last forever.

Every cyborg stood still, as if they were rooted to the floor. Some had their mouths open as disbelief flashed in their shining eyes.

Emotions suffocated Phoebe, making it difficult to breathe as everything got stuck in her throat. Her eyes saw what Faye was doing, but she had a hard time believing it. Hadn't Faye heard her say what would happen if she touched one of the cyborgs in an intimate way?

For a split second, she'd seen fear in Silver's eyes. He'd known what was coming as Faye had pressed her lips to his. He'd struggled, tried to get away, but that had only lasted a few seconds.

Now, he stood like a statue, arms at his sides, trance-like, and not moving. His eyes stared into the blue.

Then, they flashed.

It was strong and bright, as if someone had turned on a flashlight for a split second.

"Fuck!" Hunter yelled. "His eyes flashed!"

That got every Fighter moving.

Shade remained on the floor, held down by Edge and Hunter.

"Get her away from him!" Nightmare roared.

A dark-haired Fighter grabbed Faye by the waist and pulled her away from Silver. He pushed her back into the cage and closed the door, earning a long chant of curse words.

Silver stood emotionless, his empty gaze still looking far into the distance.

Nightmare stepped around Shade, Hunter, and Edge, and approached Silver. "Get him on the gurney," he ordered Hunter and Edge.

Edge retrieved the syringe and removed the plastic safety. He stuck Shade's arm.

Phoebe's throat tightened from the sight, suffocating her scream.

Nightmare turned Silver toward him. He examined him before he turned to Heaven. "How many times did his eyes flash?"

"Only once," the blond Fighter answered.

Nightmare took a deep breath and exhaled audibly, but his eyes hardened when he looked at Faye. "Congratulations. You've just bound a cyborg to yourself."

Faye glared. "At least I got you to stop beating up on Shade."

"Is that why you did it? Have you lost your mind?"

189

"It was worth it."

Nightmare snorted. "We'll see if you still believe that in a few minutes."

Phoebe watched Shade who lay motionless on the floor. His eyes were closed. Her body trembled. Her knees felt weak and tears ran down her cheeks as Hunter and Edge put him onto the gurney.

"Take him to the car and tie him down," Nightmare told two Fighters and pointed at Silver. "Make sure he won't be able to get free."

They grabbed Silver's arms and led him from the house. He still seemed far away and didn't protest.

Nightmare approached the gurney where Shade lay. He grabbed the straps and tied them around Shade's wrists and legs with determination.

"Please, don't do it," Phoebe begged. "Don't take him away from me."

Nightmare ignored her. He snatched the cords attached to the machine and placed them on Shade's forehead and temples. He opened her cyborg's shirt and put the last two on his chest.

The machine buzzed quietly, freaking Phoebe out more with all its blinking lights and computer-like sounds. It beeped from time to time. Sometimes, it was just one beep, another time it was a whole sequence, as if it was repeating a pattern.

Nightmare looked Shade over. Then he studied the machine before his gaze turned to Edge who stood by the machine again. "Ready?"

The Fighter nodded.

Nightmare finally looked at her. "We're making history, Phoebe. You should be proud. Yours and Shade's sacrifice will save the entire race of cyborgs."

She couldn't answer. Her jaw tremored too much, and the tears almost blinded her.

"You'll regret this," Wind growled.

"What I will regret is not trying." Nightmare turned to Edge again. "Turn it on."

Edge pressed a button.

CHAPTER 27

Darkness surrounded him. It was peaceful and quiet, but slowly, the world in the distance became clearer.

Something went on around him, but he couldn't grasp what. A thick wall was between him and whatever was on the other side.

Voices reached his ears. At first, they made no sense. He couldn't make out a single word, but after a while, a woman's voice came through.

She was crying and sounded upset.

His mind wanted to slip back into the silence and the calmness, but the woman pulled him in the other direction.

Her voice was so familiar.

She wasn't talking directly to him, but she pulled him toward her with her sweet presence. His heart whispered her name over and over again.

Phoebe ...

Shade wanted to reach for her but couldn't move. He could barely feel his limbs.

The darkness still held him in a firm grip. He couldn't pull himself out of it. All he knew was he *had* to. His mind

192

was foggy. Everything was so far away. So muffled.

Someone touched him. It wasn't a nice touch. It was firm and unpleasant. Strong hands wrapped something around his wrists, then his feet.

The first words hit his ears.

"What I will regret is not trying." It was Nightmare's dark voice. "Turn it on."

There was a click.

Pain shot through him. It was sudden, sharp, and attacked every nerve ending in his brain. He threw back his head, clenched his fists, and struggled against every muscle in his body. He jerked his eyes open and stared up at the roof as the agony made him cry out.

"Shade!"

Phoebe's desperate call echoed in his head.

"He's awake!" Edge yelled.

Shade noticed a dark figure on the other side of him before the pain almost blinded him. He screamed again.

In the distance, Phoebe screamed with him.

"What?" Nightmare yelled. "How is that even possible? Didn't you give him the serum?"

"I did," Edge barked back.

"He should be out for hours," Nightmare growled. "Change the sequence."

It felt like every part of his brain was under attack by sharp needles. They stung him, invaded every part of him. His cybernetics protested, and it didn't take long for them to recognize what caused the pain.

A signal.

The thing Nightmare had been talking about.

The thing that would remove his bond to Phoebe.

The signal tried to break into his programming, it tried to take over.

Fear rushed him, and he roared. It wasn't just trying to remove his bond to Phoebe.

It was trying to make him forget her.

"Sequence changed," Edge said.

Pain subsided, and Shade relaxed. He was out of breath, his muscles ached, and he felt bruised all over. His body was covered with sweat and his heart pounded.

He still felt stinging inside his brain. Thankfully, it didn't hurt anymore, but it was uncomfortable.

The signal was like a virus. MedAct had given him advance protection shields from things like this, but it was intelligent and sophisticated. It knew what it was looking for. Keeping it out of his programming was almost impossible.

"He's struggling," Edge said.

Nightmare leaned over Shade. "Of course he is. He is trying to protect himself." He looked at Edge. "You know what to do."

Buttons were pushed.

A pressure filled his head. It invaded every part of his brain, attacking his programming and cybernetics again and again, trying to convince him to let go.

Shade roared in discomfort.

The Fighters leader leaned over him again. "The more

you fight, the more you're hurting yourself."

Shade gave him a glare as his body quivered. "Never. You're not just trying to break my bond to Phoebe. You're trying to make me forget her."

"Yes." There was sadness in his eyes. "That's the only way. To break the bond, I must delete every trace of it."

Shade bared his teeth. "I won't let you."

Nightmare didn't look away from him when he said; "Edge!"

"I'm on it."

Shade heard buttons being pressed again, and a second later, the pressure inside his head intensified. Shade groaned as he threw back his head and arched his back.

Phoebe cried out again, calling his name.

The pain in her voice made his heart ache.

He was failing her.

The signal searched inside him. It broke down his defenses and kept pressing forward to gain access to his advanced program. One wrong move and it would succeed. It would change him forever.

It would take Phoebe away from him.

But keeping it out wore him out.

He was so tired.

His body trembled and a shaky groan left his mouth.

"A little bit more, Edge," Nightmare said.

Buttons were pushed once more.

The pressure eased up in most places inside his head. Instead, it focused on one spot only.

That could only mean one thing.

The signal had found what it was searching for.

Fear filled him when his defenses started to break down. He tried to push it away, to lock it out using his protection shields, but they didn't work.

The signal was too strong.

He knew what would happen if it gained access to that part of his brain. That was where the most important part of his programming was. Everything that was him, everything that Phoebe wanted him to be was there, but as a cyborg, he was also part human meaning he could choose to ignore the programming that she'd given him and turn into his own, unique person.

Shade had never seen the need to ignore the programming because he'd been happy with how things were. But Nightmare's invading signal would force him to become someone he wasn't, someone he didn't want to be.

It would take away the bond to Phoebe. He would forget her, and by doing so, it would shut down who he was.

"Almost there," Edge said.

A furious roar was heard from the outside before something slammed into the wall of the house.

Nightmare and Edge jerk away and looked toward the entrance door.

"What was that?" Faye asked.

Something was going on outside. Grunts, groans, and things being dragged around on the ground were heard. Seconds later, the door was forced open.

"Silver has gotten free!" a Fighter yelled, "and we're about to have company. MedAct's cyborg soldiers will be here within five minutes."

"Fuck!" Nightmare cursed, pacing around the gurney.

Shade had a hard time focusing on what was going on further away from him. The signal was minutes from breaking through. Every word, every move, and every sound felt like it came from far away.

"Grab our things and return to the base with Silver. Edge, Hunter, Heaven, and I will stay behind to see this through," Nightmare told someone.

Silver hollered from outside. He seemed to be close to the door.

"Oh, my God," Faye gasped. "What's wrong with him?"

Shade closed his eyes and tried to focus on the invasive signal, but their words still reached him.

"I'm guessing he's pissed off at you for kissing him, but he's trying to get to you to finish what you started. I doubt he wants to, but you didn't give him much choice. His bond is screaming inside him to finish the bonding process," Nightmare said.

"Damn it, I just kissed him to break up the fighting." Faye sounded scared.

"You were told what would happen if you touched one of us intimately."

"I guess I didn't take it seriously. It sounded too weird."

"And that proves you don't have much of a brain. You bonded a cyborg to yourself whether you intended to do it

197

or not. He'll do everything in his power now to reach you. He'll never give up until he is completely bonded to you. I might be able to drag him away from here today, but mark my words, he *will* come for you, and you won't be able to run away. He *will* finish the bonding process and the only way to do that is through intercourse. He will fall deeper and deeper in love with you." He took a deep breath. "And you know what? He will hate you for it."

Someone stormed into the room, breaking Shade's concentration. A loud roar filled his ears before something smashed into a wall. A groan of pain followed by quick footsteps. More groans. Something broke. It sounded like wood, maybe a chair.

The final part of his protective shield crumbled into pieces. The signal had free access to his programming now. There was nothing he could do to stop it from doing what it was designed for.

"Don't let him come near me!" Faye yelled.

There were more screaming, roaring, and another something being dragged around on the floor before he heard the sound of something hitting the wall again.

"Sedate him before he wrecks the place!" Nightmare yelled. "Keep him away from the cage and from Shade."

He heard more noises, but it was difficult to tell them apart. The signal sent thousands of tiny inputs into his mind, slowly taking the bond's place.

A deep emotional hole grew inside his chest. It was strong enough to break his heart.

Strong enough to kill him.

Nightmare's signal couldn't fill that hole, and as it grew bigger, it ripped out more and more of his soul, taking his reason for living away.

Phoebe.

He screamed louder as he writhed on the gurney. Shade threw his head from one side to the other as he desperately tried to get free.

He was losing her, one memory after another. There was nothing but darkness and emptiness where he should have a memory. And now, he also knew Nightmare's signal was failing. It wasn't setting him free from the bond.

It was killing him.

The signal would never be able to replace the bond and fill that emotional hole inside Shade's chest. Instead, his bond would think his bound one had died, didn't matter if she stood just a few feet from him.

An image from the very first time he saw her flashed by.

He'd been lying on a bed and she'd leaned over him. Phoebe had smiled ... her eyes had been so gentle and filled with love ...

... and then she faded away ...

CHAPTER 28

Phoebe stared at Silver. He'd been wrestled to the floor by the other Fighters, but his gaze was set on Faye. He'd gone crazy after storming the house, destroying everything in his way to reach Faye, but the Fighters hadn't let him.

Faye stood behind Wind with fear in her eyes. She peeked out from behind him to look at Silver.

"Hurry up," Nightmare growled and looked at the Fighters. "All of you, and Silver, must be gone before MedAct's cyborg soldiers show up."

A red-haired Fighter pulled out a syringe. The cyborg stabbed Silver's arm and emptied the liquid into him.

Silver groaned. His gaze was still set on Faye as his body slowly started to fail him. He eventually exhaled heavily, closed his eyes, and remained still on the floor.

The Fighters who held him breathed out and got to their feet. Several of them glared at Faye, but no one said anything. Instead, they lifted the unconscious Silver and left the house.

A minute later, Phoebe heard a car leaving. Only Nightmare, Edge, Hunter, and Heaven remained.

Hunter approached the gurney. "We should leave, too."

"I need a few more minutes. We're so close. It's in his system now. The answer should come any second." Nightmare watched Shade intently.

"I doubt you have those minutes."

Nightmare didn't answer, nor did he take his eyes off Shade.

Phoebe's heart ached as she watched the man she loved lay still on the gurney.

His eyes were closed. He'd stopped fighting. His head had slumped to the side, but his chest rose and fell as he breathed. That gave her some comfort. At least, he was still alive, but in what condition?

She had no idea how Nightmare tried to remove the bond. All she saw was that damn machine that stood by the gurney. Its cords were attached to Shade. She heard it beep from time to time, but neither Nightmare nor Edge touched it anymore.

Her eyes were swollen from all the crying and her throat sore from all the yelling. It hadn't mattered what she'd said. Nightmare had ignored her completely, and Wind's attempt to comfort her hadn't helped either.

He was a great friend but seeing Shade like this made her inconsolable.

Faye wasn't her usual brave self either anymore. She stood silently in the cage and wrung her hands together as she took one deep breath after another. Phoebe could only imagine what was going through her mind.

Minutes seemed to pass by. No one said anything as Edge and Nightmare watched Shade's motionless body. What finally broke the silence was the sound of approaching cars.

The door to the house was open since the Fighters had left with Silver. They hadn't bothered closing it.

None of them moved, but their gazes turned to the door.

Heaven stood by the cage along with Hunter while Edge and Nightmare remained by the gurney.

Engines died before the sound of opening and closing car doors was heard. Then there was silence again.

Hope gripped Phoebe. This would be over soon.

Edge shut down the machine and removed the cords from Shade's body. Then, he slammed his hand right through the machine.

Phoebe jerked, expecting Nightmare to get furious, but he didn't move an inch. Instead, he watched Edge in silence. Finally, Nightmare nodded, and Phoebe understood. They didn't want the machine to end up in MedAct's hands, but what about Shade? Why wasn't he waking up?

Approaching steps preceded Jade's entrance. She was followed by two muscular and scary-looking cyborgs. They were dressed in black and held big, black rifles in their hands, pointing them directly at the Fighters in the room.

Jade's eyes narrowed as she made eye-contact with him. "Nightmare," she said with a cold voice.

He took a few steps away from the gurney. "Doctor Jade Silva. I didn't expect to see you here."

"Of course, you didn't." Jade turned her gaze to the cage.

"Let them go."

Nightmare's features darkened. "Why should I listen to you?"

Phoebe had never seen Jade this cold before, but her strong posture told her that the doctor knew what she was doing. She didn't look the slightest bit scared of Nightmare or the situation.

Nightmare hated the doctor, and planned to kill her, but did Jade know that? Probably not. If they got out of here alive, she promised herself to tell Jade everything.

Jade shrugged. "Well, you don't have to if you don't want to, but if you don't, these guys will pump you full of lead. The choice is yours."

Nightmare stiffened and looked like he wanted to strangle her. Eventually, he nodded to Hunter.

Hunter approached the cage and opened the door.

Phoebe lunged for Shade.

Edge moved out of her way. He didn't stop her, and neither did Nightmare.

Her tears had run dry, but her heart still ached. The pain inside her chest was excruciating. From the corner of her eye, she noticed Wind leading Faye toward the entrance door.

Jade approached the gurney. "What have you done to him?"

Nightmare didn't answer.

Phoebe answered for him. "They tried to remove the bond."

"What?" Jade glared at Nightmare. "Have you lost your mind? Why would you want to do that?"

Without a warning, Nightmare invaded her personal space, but Jade didn't move.

The cyborg soldiers near the entrance door reacted and turned their rifles at Nightmare.

Jade raised her hand, telling them to back down.

The cyborg soldiers remained still but didn't lower their rifles.

Phoebe shook Shade, but there was no reaction. "Please, he needs help."

Nightmare didn't move.

"You heard her. Get out of my way," Jade said.

"He'll wake up when his reprogramming is done."

"What kind of reprogramming?"

Nightmare grinned. "You're the scientist, you figure it out."

They glared at each other.

Their staring contest started to get on Phoebe's nerves.

"You're killing him," Jade stated.

Nightmare growled. "I'm saving him. When he wakes up, the bond will no longer drive him. He'll have no memory of his bound one. He'll be free to choose his own life. He'll be free from the likes of *you*."

Shade suddenly screamed. He writhed on the gurney, throwing his head back and forward.

Jade pushed herself around Nightmare and approached the gurney. She took a small device from her bag and pulled out two cords from it. "I wouldn't attempt stopping me," she told Nightmare without looking at him. "Remember the lead."

His shining eyes radiated pure hatred, but he didn't move from his spot.

Phoebe was glad to see how powerless Nightmare was right now. If he tried anything, the cyborg soldiers would shoot him, and that would be the end of him. Phoebe didn't feel sorry for him one bit.

None of the other Fighters moved. They watched their leader with emotionless eyes.

"Get them out of here," Jade said as she attached the cords to Shade's temples.

The cyborg soldiers obeyed, and more entered the house.

To Phoebe's surprise, they went quietly. She'd expected more resistance considering they'd chosen to stay behind, or maybe they just didn't want to die.

She watched Jade work with an unpleasant feeling in her stomach.

The doctor's fingers flew around on the small screen of the device.

Phoebe felt so helpless. There was nothing she could do for Shade. Watching him writhe in pain shredded her apart on the inside.

"That bastard," Jade hissed.

Phoebe jerked. "What? What is it?"

"He's trying to replace the bond with another signal, but it's not working. Shade's dying. The signal is not capable of replacing the bond. He needs to be taken back to MedAct at once. There is nothing I can do for him here. I'll sedate him for now and lower his heart rate. That will slow the signal's progress."

Phoebe swallowed. "Nightmare was so sure."

"I don't give a damn what he thought he was. He *will* pay for this."

"Can you save him?" she pleaded, stifling a sob.

Jade hesitated. "I don't know." She pushed a few buttons on the screen and Shade relaxed. He stopped screaming. "I will do everything in my power to save him, but there's a risk he'll never be the same again."

Her words awakened a huge cocktail of everything from hope to despair within Phoebe. "Nightmare believes cyborgs can live without the bond." Phoebe's chin trembled. "Can they?"

Jade frowned. "I have no idea where he got that idea from. The bond is what their programming is based on. Without it, they can't exist."

Confusion struck Phoebe. "But Nightmare said he existed before he was bound and that the doctor, Carolyn Williams, bound him to her years after his creation."

Jade snorted. "All these years as a Fighter must have messed with his mind." She removed the cords from Shade's temples and put the device back into her bag. "Wait here. I'll call for a helicopter." Jade left the house.

Everything suddenly became very quiet.

Phoebe lay her head on Shade's warm, muscled chest,

feeling his soft skin against her cheek. She'd never been religious, but at this moment, she felt the need to pray. "Please, don't take him away from me." Her tears ran down on him, wetting his skin. "Stay with me .... please ..."

CHAPTER 29

Shade lay on the hospital bed inside MedAct's walls. His eyes were closed. His breathing was slow but stable.

Three days had passed since they'd left that awful house. Three nerve-wracking days, and Shade hadn't awakened yet.

Jade and her team of doctors had done everything in their power to save him, but not even she knew what would happen once Shade woke. The bond had been damaged and the doctor had warned her he'd probably never be the same again.

The bond was as fragile as a vase that'd been dropped to the floor. It could be put together again, but the vase would never look whole again. The cracks would always be there.

What if his feelings were gone? Would she be able to let him go?

Just the thought of it almost broke her heart.

"You need to relax, Phoebe," Faye said. "You're not doing yourself a favor worrying this much."

Phoebe looked at Faye who sat on a chair. There were four other chairs in the room, and three of them were occupied by Wind, Diane, and Celise. They'd all been there for her and Shade, and Phoebe couldn't be more grateful.

"I know." She sighed. "I can't help it, though. I just wish he would wake up."

"He will wake up. That much Jade was sure of," Diane assured her.

So many things had changed since the time in the house. Wind had been a great support for both her and Faye after they'd left.

It had helped Faye to get back to herself, but she wasn't as vocal anymore. Worry now shone in her eyes.

Phoebe ran her hand down her face. "I never believed things would turn out like this. It feels like pure chaos. I thought it was over, but then Nightmare and his Fighters managed to flee from the cyborg soldiers before they could bring them in. Hunter didn't get away, but the others are still out there and who knows what they're planning. Nightmare will want Shade back. This is far from over."

There was an unpleasant silence.

"I don't think Nightmare will bother with Shade anymore," Wind finally said.

She shot him a look. "Why do you think that?"

"Because the bond has been damaged. Even if Nightmare doesn't know that, I think he can figure it out. Shade can no longer help Nightmare with his so-called quest."

Wind's words were calming but there was no guarantee. Maybe Nightmare would come after Shade again but worrying about it right now only made her headache worse.

Faye was right. She needed to relax.

The door opened, and Jade entered.

She was dressed in her doctor coat and her hair was in a ponytail.

Jade smiled at everyone and approached the bed. She leaned over Shade and looked him over for a moment before she turned her focus to the machine that stood on the other side of the bed. Different numbers and complicated words flashed by on its screen from time to time. "No change."

Everyone approached her.

"Is that a good thing?" Phoebe asked.

"Yes. It means he's stable. He should wake up any minute. When his cybernetics and programming have accepted the changes we've done, he'll open his eyes. We have restored your bond to our best ability, but his programming will believe he isn't bound, but don't worry. He'll recognize you."

Hope awakened within Phoebe.

"What about Nightmare?" Diane asked.

Jade took a deep breath. "I don't know. They managed to escape, as you know, but we have Hunter. We won't make the same mistake with him as we did with Silver. Hunter will remain here until he's bound again. We already have the right woman for him."

Faye snorted. "He'll be pissed."

"He will, but he'll calm down when he sees who it is."

"Who is it?" Phoebe asked.

Jade smiled. "Someone from his past. She has agreed to help him." Her gaze locked onto Shade, but she spoke to them all. "I've listened to everything you've told me. You've given me an insight into the Fighters lives. They rarely talk to us when we get our hands on them. The few things we know are not enough for us to understand them."

"How about what Nightmare said. Is the bond ... a lie?"

Jade gave her a gaze filled with understanding. "No, Phoebe. The bond is as real as your love for Shade. When you take it away, you take away a part of the cyborg, and that's what Nightmare wanted to do to Shade. I won't go into all the technical things the signal did, but I can assure you that Shade would've died if Nightmare would've been allowed to finish. How the Fighters survive after losing their bound ones is still a mystery to us, but we suspect it has something to do with the bond. Unless a Fighter agrees to be examined, we don't touch them. We don't force them to bond themselves either. We suggest it, but if they don't, they won't be set free. However, they will get good lives."

She nodded. "Is there a way for cyborgs to live without the bond?"

Everyone's gaze fell upon Jade.

The doctor sighed. "Not that I'm aware of, and believe me, I've been working here for many years. I haven't found a single indication as to whether that is even possible."

Faye tensed and swallowed loudly. "So, where does that leave Silver and me?"

Jade looked at Faye. "You kissed him, right?"

Faye nodded.

"What did he do during the kiss?"

"At first, he tried to get away, but after a few seconds, he remained still. He just stood there."

The doctor's expression tensed. "Did his eyes flash?"

"Yes, once."

"I see." Jade took a deep breath. "When a Fighter becomes bound to a new person, his eyes will flash three times as his cybernetics accepts the bond. The first flash initiates it. The second flash accepts the woman, and the third flash seals the bond. This only happens with the Fighters. How long the bonding process takes varies from cyborg to cyborg. No bonding is the same."

"So, Silver and I ...?" Faye's eyes were big and her lips tense.

"I think you already know. When you kissed him, you initiated the bond."

"Nightmare said Silver will come for me." Her words were almost a whisper.

"He will."

"Is there a way to terminate the bonding process?"

"No, but don't worry. We'll do everything we can to help you, but you must be aware of the fact that this will probably end with him completing the bonding process."

Faye's gaze hardened. "Over my dead body."

A sound came from the bed and Phoebe ignored everyone instantly.

Shade took a deep breath before he opened his eyes and stared up at the ceiling.

Joy filled her. He was awake!

But then, she tensed. This was the moment of truth.

Would he remember her? Would he still love her? Or was their bond damaged for good?

It felt like the whole room suddenly held its breath. No one moved. No one spoke.

Shade lay still for almost a whole minute before he braced himself on his arms and sat up. His gaze swept over them all before landing on Phoebe. He watched her with his emotionless, shining eyes.

Her heart thundered and it felt as if she would come apart any second if he didn't do something soon. She had to give him time, but it was going to kill her. He'd been out for days and his programming had been messed with, but her patience was wearing thin.

Phoebe swallowed and moved closer. "Shade?" She placed her shaky hand on his cheek.

His body tensed when her hand made contact with his skin. He inhaled sharply and his eyes went big.

Then they flashed.

It was so bright that it lit up parts of his face for a short second.

Another flash came.

This time it wasn't as bright.

"He's accepted you. Now, you just have to complete the bonding ... when you're alone." Jade smiled.

Phoebe's cheeks heated.

Shade closed his eyes and leaned into her touch with a big exhale.

"Shade?" she asked again, this time with hope in her voice.

"I lost you," he whispered. "They took me away from you." He opened his eyes and looked at her. "I know now what the Fighters feel. They think they're strong without the bond, but they are not. They're alive because a small part of the bond survived when their bound ones died, and that small part screams inside them all the time. It screams for love, for a bound one. It's what makes them dangerous, and it's what makes them slowly lose their minds. I got to experience that for a short time. It was the worst feeling ever and I don't ever want to feel it again. It was as if a black hole had been dug inside my chest." He grabbed Phoebe's hand and pulled her closer. Shade wrapped his arms around her waist and rested his head against her stomach. "I lost you, but my feelings for you never went away. I sense the bond has been fixed, but I need to bond with you again. I long for you so much."

Phoebe's cheeks heated even more, Shade didn't seem to care that others were present. His touch was gentle but firm, whispering of the longing that lingered in his body.

His eyes had only flashed twice.

A third time was needed to seal the bond, and she'd give him that.

"I could feel Nightmare's signal working. It was designed to remove the bond and make me forget Phoebe. It was designed to take the bond's place, but by doing so, it was also killing me. I don't think Nightmare understood the consequences of removing the bond completely."

Jade sighed. "So, it is as I suspected."

214

"I heard everything you said, Jade. Your suspicions are true; they are alive because their bonds aren't completely gone. They just refuse to accept that."

"Instead, they believe they are free."

Shade nodded. A shiver went through him and his grip on Phoebe tightened.

Jade's lips twitched. "Everyone, we need to leave. Phoebe and Shade need to be alone for a while."

Everyone gave her a wide smile and left the room without a word.

When they closed the door behind them, she looked at Shade.

He stared back at her with fire in his eyes.

CHAPTER 30

Shade could stare at her for hours. It was as if she'd bewitched him in every possible way, making him uninterested in everything around him. Unable to pull away from her, he made her straddle him.

"I was so worried," Phoebe said.

"Worried that I wouldn't wake?"

"Yes, and that you wouldn't love me anymore."

He smiled, gently pressing his hips up against hers. Their clothes and the blanket were frustratingly in the way. He needed to get close to her, as close as possible, and the need grew by the second.

He'd felt the bond react twice. It had initiated when Phoebe had touched him, and it'd accepted her just as fast. That tiny piece that remained of the bond had recognized her, and it knew what it wanted, what *he* wanted.

They just needed to seal it now.

"That's not possible," he said. "My love for you is eternal. If the bond is removed, I will die. Nightmare believes a lie if he thinks the bond is fake. It is not. It is who we are. He just refuses to accept that, but I choose happiness. I'll always choose you over what the Fighters have. I got a small taste of their pain, and I can't imagine living like that. It must be horrible." He frowned. "Nightmare has lived like that for forty years. He's trying to set himself free from himself, and that's impossible." His hand gently caressed her cheek. "I love you. Don't ever doubt that."

Tears of joy filled Phoebe's eyes. "I love you, too. I don't know what I would do without you."

"I'll never let you find out." He grinned but turned serious a few seconds later. "What did Nightmare do to you before I arrived?"

Phoebe became still. "He ... held me."

He winced, hadn't expected that answer. "He held you? He made it sound like he did a lot more."

"Don't worry. He just held me."

"Why?"

"Because he's lonely. He can't touch an unbound woman without his bond thinking he wants to bind himself to her, but he said he was safe with me."

Shade frowned. "How was he safe with you?"

"Since you're bound to me, he can touch me. His bond won't accept me as a potential bound one."

He nodded, tensing his lips.

Phoebe studied him. "Are you ... angry with me?"

"Why would I be angry at you? He didn't give you a choice, did he?"

"No. I couldn't get away from him."

"Of course, you couldn't. He's a cyborg." His gaze

darkened. "But if I ever see him again, he'll pay for everything he's done to us."

She touched his cheek. "I hope that day will never come. The last thing I want is to see you hurt again. I want this to be over, and I pray that Nightmare has lost all interest in you, just like Wind assumed." Phoebe wrapped her arms around him.

Her warmth and feminine scent filled his senses. "Bond with me." His voice was a whisper filled with pleasurable promises.

"You don't have to ask me twice." She pressed her lips against his.

Shade couldn't stop the moan from escaping his mouth.

He'd make love to his one and only, and they'd seal the bond anew. He'd show her how much she meant to him. Their love was true and real, no matter what Nightmare said. Shade felt it in his entire being, and he knew she felt it too.

TEMPTED CYBORG

WHEN THE PAST COMES HIS WAY,
HE CAN'T HELP BUT FACE IT.

When Avril Davis was a child, the cyborg Hunter lived with his bound one in her neighborhood. He used to babysit her, but that was twenty years ago. Things are different now. Hunter's bound one is dead and he's one of the Fighters. He's nothing like the Hunter she once knew.

Being caught by MedAct is a fate Hunter never saw coming, but he sees what's in store for him now. The doctors want him to bind himself again. They even have a woman in mind. He promises himself to do everything he can to make the woman change her mind. He's going to make sure she'll never want anything to do with him. That is at least until Avril Davis walks back into his life...

CHAPTER 1

Avril looked through the one-way window into the interrogation room, where Doctor Jade Silva and another doctor stood next to a table. She'd talked to Jade a lot over the past two weeks. The other one she didn't know, but he was a middle-aged man with a bright beard and kind eyes.

The walls in the room were white, and by the small table, sat a Fighter. He was cuffed to it, but the cuffs weren't regular ones. These were thicker, specially designed for cyborgs. He also seemed drugged, judging by his slack sitting position.

Avril licked her lips as she watched the Fighter. His intimidating persona made her heart pound. His dark glare said not to mess with him. He had to be at least six feet five tall, and his muscular frame didn't ease the impression of him.

She could barely stand still. The adrenaline pumped in her body.

Her entire life might change today.

"Good evening, Hunter," Jade said. "How are you feeling?" The doctor was dressed in a white coat and she held a block of papers in her hands. Her dark hair was put up into a ponytail.

"Piss off," he growled.

"As positive as always, I see."

Hunter.

Memories from the past flashed through Avril's mind. It'd been twenty years, but she still remembered him. He'd been so different back then. He'd been happy, always smiling. She'd never had a reason to be afraid of him, but now, she did. He wasn't the same anymore. Hunter was now marked by a tough life.

Avril had been twelve the day it happened. She'd been out playing with her friends in their neighborhood, in the southern part of Glaswell.

Hunter and his bound one, Sarah, had lived on the other side of the street.

Sarah had been outside, packing the trunk of their car when Avril had heard the sounds of squeaking wheels from an approaching vehicle. She'd barely managed to turn around before she'd spotted a black, huge truck driving way too fast toward Sarah.

Seconds later, it'd hit Sarah straight on, pinning her against the car. The sound from the impact had been deafening and had sent chills through Avril.

Sarah hadn't had a chance. She'd died immediately.

Her death had devastated Hunter. Avril and the other children had watched him go crazy once he'd realized what'd happened. He'd completely lost it, roaring out his pain and desperation as he'd ripped the driver from the truck. He'd been a middle-aged man with glazed eyes.

Avril had assumed he'd been drunk.

Hunter had snapped his neck before falling to the ground in spasms.

A few minutes later, cyborgs, police, ambulance, and other people had shown up. They'd taken Hunter away and that had been the last time she'd seen him.

Until now.

Avril's heart clenched as she watched him. There was so much hate in his beautiful shining eyes. He was still as handsome as she remembered, but now, he looked worn out. He needed to shave and a change of clothes.

Jade had informed her that Hunter had been given food, a place to stay, and clothing, but he'd just paced inside his room, looking for a way out, ignoring the clothes and the food. He was starving himself and that broke Avril's heart.

Today, she was here because she hoped she'd be able to help him. There were no guarantees, but she'd do everything in her power to help him.

MedAct had a special program for the Fighters they caught. The program intended to give them a good life again, with a new bound one.

Women who wanted to help could sign up. They were put in school and went through tons of medical, mental, and physical tests before they were either approved, or denied, to become the new bound one of a Fighter.

Fighters weren't like newborn cyborgs. They wore deep

scars and dark histories in their hearts. They needed a firm, but gentle hand. They needed women strong enough to handle them.

Most women who signed up for the program couldn't afford a cyborg of their own, and Avril was one of them. Working as a waitress would never give her enough money to apply for a cyborg.

She'd waited for this day ever since she'd been approved. It'd been two years since that day. She'd signed up when she'd learned that Hunter had survived and become one of the Fighters. She didn't know how he'd joined them, but it didn't matter.

She'd signed up in hopes he'd be found one day. The chance had been slim, but here he was. Miracles did happen, and she promised herself she wouldn't screw this up.

Avril hugged herself and tried to calm her rushing heart as she listened to the conversation in the interrogation room.

"You haven't eaten for almost two days, Hunter," Jade said.

He flashed his teeth and growled. "Let me go and you won't have to watch me starve to death."

"I wish you'd see reason. We're not going to hurt you. There's no need to torment yourself. Starvation only puts more pressure on your already stressed body."

He snorted. "I'm not stressed."

The doctor frowned. "Your heart rate is up. You barely sleep, and now, you're refusing to eat. You're growing weaker by the minute, so don't lie to me."

Hunter glared but didn't say anything.

Jade sighed. "I'll make sure something is brought to you, and you won't leave this room until you've finished your plate."

Avril didn't like the hate she saw in his eyes. Would he look at her the same way? Would he even recognize her? She had no idea, but it wouldn't be easy. There was no guarantee she'd be able to make him look at her the way she wished he would.

The cyborg she wanted leaned forward in his chair. "Then we're going to be here for a long time."

Jade snickered. "I doubt it. I'll bring in everything I know you love to eat. You can then either torture yourself by staring at the food as it gets cold, or enjoy it before you're brought back to your room."

The other doctor wrote something down before he turned to Jade. "I'll go and inform the kitchen."

She nodded. "Check his files for what he likes to eat."

Avril took a deep breath as she watched him go. Soon, it'd be her turn. Nerves were eating her up from the inside out, but she had a plan.

Cyborgs had an amazing memory, but there was no guarantee he'd remember her. She'd changed over the twenty years. She wasn't the child he used to babysit anymore. She'd grown up. She was all woman.

He'd never left her mind. He'd always been there with her, every day of her life. Taking part in everything Avril did, whether she wanted or not. She'd never been able to let him go, and now when she was here, it was the best day of her life. But at the same time, the most nervous one.

"Please," she whispered to herself. "Don't let him hate me."

Avril lowered her head and looked at the red rose in her hand. Would it help him remember her?

The day before Sarah had died, she'd given him a red rose. She'd been worried, but he'd accepted the rose with a smile. It'd been her silly, little way to show him she liked him. In her twelve-year-old and naive mind, she'd hoped he'd see her crush for him, but he never had.

Today, she knew why. Today, Avril knew how the bond worked.

She raised her head again and kept watching Hunter.

"I won't touch your poisoned food," he growled.

Jade raised an eyebrow. "Do you seriously believe we'd poison your food?"

His gaze darkened. "How else do you manage to keep me drugged? I can barely think straight."

"You're drugged in your sleep. That way no harm comes to you or us."

"So, you just enter my room when I sleep and drug me?"

"No, not me. Other cyborgs."

Hunter snorted. "Of course."

"So please, eat the food."

Yet again, he didn't say anything. Silence filled the interrogation room.

"Let's make a deal," the doctor said after a while. "I'll

stop drugging you if you start eating, but if you try to escape, or if you hurt anyone, the drugs *will* return within seconds. Am I making myself clear?"

He seemed to ponder her suggestion. Minutes felt like hours, until he finally nodded. "Fine."

Jade smiled. "Good." She wrote something down. "Food will be brought here within half an hour. Eat it, and you'll wake up with a clear mind tomorrow."

His gaze narrowed. "You're giving me the chance to escape, you know that, don't you?"

"Yes, but I'm also trying to show you, you can trust me. No one here will hurt you. We only want what's best for you. What's safe for you."

He snorted again. "Safety, my ass. You only do it because it will give you fewer problems."

"Think what you want."

"I want to eat in my room," he demanded. "I don't want to sit here and wait."

"You won't have to."

Suspicious filled his gaze. "What are you talking about?"

"You're going to meet someone." Jade grinned and left the room.

CHAPTER 2

Avril saw confusion in Hunter's beautiful eyes as Jade left the interrogation room. Seconds later, she joined Avril.

The doctor smiled. "Are you ready?"

She clenched her fists. "No."

"Everything will be all right, and if something goes wrong, the cyborg soldiers will be by your side within seconds." She nodded toward the two male cyborgs who stood inside the room.

They were much taller than a human man could ever become with muscular and intimidating bodies. Their gazes were serious, and Avril couldn't help but wonder if they ever smiled. They were cyborg soldiers, specially designed to protect those who worked for MedAct. She'd no idea how many they were, but each one of them was bound to a doctor or other personnel.

She looked through the one-way window again and studied Hunter. He looked tense with his gaze fixed on the door. She'd no idea who he expected to walk through it, but his clenched expression told her he probably expected his worst nightmare.

"I have faith in you, Avril," Jade said. "If anyone can make Hunter bind himself again it's you. Besides, you two already know each other, and that will help a lot."

Her hands trembled. "I hope so." She'd no idea if she trusted her own words or not. "I will not give up on him."

"I know you won't." The doctor put her papers on the desk. "But before you go in there, I need to tell you a few things."

Surprise filled her. "Tell me what?"

Jade's gaze turned serious. The doctor was small and attractive, but the strength she radiated said she wasn't to be taken lightly. This woman knew what she wanted and how to get it.

"We managed to receive new information about the Fighters a few days ago. We don't want to spread the information before we're sure it's true. Therefore, I'd appreciate if you could help us figure it out."

Avril inhaled deeply. She hadn't expected that. "Figure out what?"

"The Fighters rarely allow us to investigate them, meaning we can't study them to learn what goes on, on the inside. We drug them to keep them calm, but we never do more than that. We don't want them as enemies. We want them to understand we mean no harm. Because of that, we don't know much about them. It's our loss, I know, but we prefer to have it that way. It's best for us all."

She nodded. "So what do you want me to do?"

"Up until now, we've believed the Fighters become

unstable because they lose the bond when their bound one dies, but now, it looks like a small part of the bond survives. That's probably why they're still alive, but their programming doesn't interpret the remaining of the bond as a bond anymore. We believe it interprets the bond as a malfunction and wants to repair it. To do that, it needs to find a new bound one. The Fighters programming tells them they need to get bound again as soon as possible. It screams inside them and if they touch an unbound woman, their programming will think they want to bind themselves again. When that happens, the bonding process initiates and that is why they never touch an unbound woman." Jade looked at Hunter, who still seemed taut. "As you know it varies from Fighter to Fighter how complicated the new bonding is. Their eyes flash three times during that time. The first flash initiates the bond, the second flash accepts it, and the final flash seals it." She looked at her. "You need to go through all that with Hunter, but I want you to find out if any of the things I've just told you are true."

Avril's heart thundered. "How am I supposed to do that?"

"One intimate touch should initiate the bonding process. If it's true, his eyes will flash as you kiss him, hug him, or do anything intimate with him. Just don't force the touch upon him. He'll hate you for it and we don't want that."

"And if he doesn't want my touch?"

"Then it might be another sign that the theory is true." She nodded. "I understand."

"You think you can find out more about it?"

"I'll try."

Avril swallowed. As if trying to become Hunter's new bound one wasn't hard enough. Now, Jade wanted her to find out more about the Fighters. There was no guarantee Hunter would ever open up to her.

"You've all the time in the world, Avril."

All she could do was nod as she took a deep breath. The moment had finally come. The moment where either all her dreams came true, or the moment where everything broke into thousands of pieces.

Her legs moved on their own as she left the room and approached the interrogation room. Her palms were warm and her knees weak. So much time had passed since they'd last seen each other, and all she could do was hope he'd recognize her.

She put her hand on the handle and slowly pressed it down. What did he feel at this moment? Was he as tense and nervous as she was? Or was he ready to fight for his life?

Avril looked down at the floor as she entered. The rose was still firmly in her grasp. She didn't dare to look up, to look into his eyes as she closed the door behind her. A deafening silence lingered in the room. She could almost hear her own heart race.

After a few nerve-wracking seconds, she finally dared to look at him.

He watched her intently.

She didn't see anger, but surprise was written all over his

233

face. Did he recognize her?

His gaze lingered down her body and to her hands. More surprise crossed his expression when he spotted the rose.

Hope awakened within her. Maybe he *did* recognize her. She gave him a gentle smile and took a step closer to the table. His posture instantly hardened and his gaze darkened. Avril froze.

"Who are you?" he asked with a deep and threatening voice.

Her tummy fell.

She'd hoped in vain. He had no idea who she was. He didn't recognize her, but she couldn't blame him. After all, it'd been twenty years, and he'd probably never thought of her during all that time.

Avril wasn't the child he'd once known. Judging by his wrecked appearance, he'd had other things on his mind. But at the same time, she couldn't get away from the pain it caused. "My name is Avril."

He raised an eyebrow. "Avril?"

She smiled again as she approached the table. She didn't want to make any sudden moves. Hunter could interpret that the wrong way.

Avril stopped in front of the table and laid the rose on it. She didn't dare to give it to him directly. She'd heard Jade's words about the bonding process initiating from one intimate touch. Would that happen if she accidentally touched him as she gave him the flower even if it wasn't an intimate touch? She had no idea, but wouldn't risk it.

"This is for you." She pushed the flower closer to him.

He picked it up and studied it before shooting her a dark gaze. "Is this some kind of joke?"

She tried not to show that his words hurt. Didn't the rose trigger some kind of memory in him? "No, no joke." She pulled out the chair and sat down.

"Then why are you giving me a rose?"

Avril watched him for a while. Her heart was almost unwilling to calm. Her chin trembled, making it difficult to talk, but somehow, she managed to form words and speak without sounding too afraid or too desperate.

Her entire body was weak from being this close to him. Thankfully, she was sitting. There was no telling when her knees would've given out if she'd still been standing. Hunter had always made a deep impact on her. As a child, her innocent crush on him had ruled her daydreams. Over the years, he'd become a memory she'd always turned to whenever she'd needed comfort.

He'd always understood her; always been there for her, as a friend. He'd made her feel like someone had actually cared about her.

Her childhood had been lonely. Her parents had taken care of her, but they'd been passive. They'd never spoken to her about all those things a child needed to talk about. They'd never done anything with her. Their dinners had mostly been silent, or filled with pointless discussions, but Hunter had given her all those things she'd so desperately needed from an adult.

Someone who'd listened, someone who'd understood. Sarah had always been there, too.

Today, Avril understood that Hunter and Sarah had known what her life had been like because they'd never told her "no". They'd made time for her, and she couldn't have been more grateful.

Then Sarah had died and Hunter had been taken away by MedAct. The most important people in her life were gone, and it had devastated her. But now, Hunter was back, and Avril would do anything to make him stay. She'd return the favor. She'd save his life, just like he'd once saved hers.

He lowered his gaze to the rose and studied it before he looked at her again. "You say your name is Avril?"

She nodded. Tears gathered behind her eyes when his face relaxed and a gentle smile revealed on his kissable lips.

"You're not a child anymore."

Avril returned his smile and dried away the tear that'd run down her cheek. "No, I'm not."

Hunter looked her over. It sent a wave of nervousness through her. Did he like what he saw? She wasn't one of the fittest women out there, but she wasn't fat or anything. Makeup didn't decorate her face either, and her dark brown hair hung down her shoulders.

"You've grown into an attractive woman, Avril." His expression was serious, making her believe he meant it.

Heat rushed to her face. "Thank you."

He reclined in the chair. "Why are you here?"

"I heard you'd been brought in and I needed to see you.

You've been in my thoughts ever since..." Avril didn't finish. She couldn't.

His smile faded. Sadness filled his eyes. "Do you work for MedAct?" He was obviously not interested in talking about the past.

"No, I don't. I work as a waitress outside of Glaswell. I'm renting a small apartment near my work."

"So life has been good to you?"

She shrugged. "It's been okay, but it's been...boring." Avril licked her lips. "I've thought of you every day since you disappeared. I was so worried. For years, I had no idea what'd happened to you. Then I heard you'd joined the Fighters. It made me happy to know you were alive, but the few photos taken of you showed you lived a tough life." She swallowed. It was difficult to talk, and her throat thickened as the tears threatened to run down her cheeks again. "I watched you turn into someone I didn't know. Every few years, new photos of you showed up, and with each photo, you looked even more marked by life. I wanted to help you just like you'd once helped me. That's why I'm here today." Avril jerked when he grabbed her hand.

His touch was warm and firm, but his eyes didn't flash. Apparently, a touch like this didn't trigger the bonding process.

"Thank you, Avril. I really appreciate you thinking of me over the years and for wanting to help me."

"You and Sarah were my whole world. You both meant to me more than you'll ever know. You kept me on my feet and gave me a purpose. And when you disappeared, you took a part of me with you."

His grip on her hand tightened and she hugged his hand back. "I'm so sorry. I didn't know."

Avril nodded. "It's okay. The important thing is that you're back, and I'm so happy to see you again."

"I'm happy to see you, too."

They looked at each other for what felt like minutes, and she couldn't help but take in his beauty. His handsome and dark features made her emotions go wild. He awakened everything she'd felt for a long time.

She'd forced herself to put him in the past and move on with her life, but now, when he sat right in front of her, it was impossible. What she felt for him now was much stronger than just a simple crush.

It had evolved into love over the years.

"So what do you do, apart from working as a waitress and running around at MedAct?" Hunter grinned.

Avril blinked, surprised that his anger had gone so fast. "Not much. I spend most of my time at home reading books, or enjoying a movie."

"Do you have someone in your life?"

Avril winced, not expecting that question. "No."

"How about your parents?"

"I have no idea. I haven't spoken to them in two years."

Hunter raised an eyebrow. "Why not?"

"Ever since I moved out, I did everything I could to stay in touch with them. But *I* was always the one making the phone calls, always the one inviting them over for dinner, or trying to make them do things with me." She sighed.

"What happened?"

"I decided to stop trying and let them take the first step." Avril went silent for a while. "I'm still waiting for them to call."

He grabbed her other hand. "If I wasn't in here, I'd take you out for dinner and a movie. I'm sure we could have a lot of fun."

Hope awoke within her.

She hadn't expected to see the old Hunter so fast, but he'd emerged as soon as he'd remembered her. It made her the happiest woman alive, but at the same time, he meant taking her out as a friend. That was all she was to him.

Avril assumed, in his mind, she was still that twelve-year-old girl who loved spending time with him and his bound one. Maybe he had a hard time seeing past that. If so, making him accept her as his next bound one would be even more difficult than she'd ever imagined. "I'd love that, and this time, we can do adult stuff instead of child stuff." Heat shot to her face and she gasped. "Um...I didn't mean..."

He laughed, and the sound hit her right in the chest, awakening all those wonderful memories she'd pushed aside.

"It's okay," Hunter said. "I understand what you mean."

"Good. It'd be rather embarrassing if you didn't." The heat on her cheeks grew and it would only get worse if she didn't change the subject. "How about you? How have you been doing?" She already had the answer, but she'd just blurted it out, searching for something to say.

His expression changed instantly. Hunter's appealing smile disappeared and his features hardened.

She'd hit a sensitive subject, and didn't expect it to be anything else. But at the same time, she wanted to know. Avril had worried herself sick about him over the years. Especially those times when she'd seen pictures of him in the media, defending himself from the police force or the cyborg soldiers. There'd been a few times when she'd believed his final moment had come. She'd cried herself to sleep those nights.

Hunter took a deep breath. "I don't remember much from the days after Sarah's death. I remember killing the driver, but after that, it's black. I remember the feelings that came over me as the bond broke. The pain, the despair. My heart had been ripped apart, and no matter what I did, I wasn't able to control it. It was so intense it made me lose consciousness on several occasions. I was dying, but then, from one minute to the other, it all just stopped. The emotional pain was still there, but hidden deep down." He placed his hand against his chest. "I can still feel it, every day of my life. I feel the damage that has been done, but I also feel how the bond is screaming for a new bound one." He took another deep breath. "After what felt like a century, I woke up in an ambulance. I was being transported somewhere. I quickly realized that I was in one of MedAct's ambulances, but I didn't want to go where ever they were taking me. To make a long story short, I managed to escape. I lingered in the woods for days until Nightmare and his Fighters found me. They made repairs to my programming, but it was far from successful. The damage was too great, but I'm still here."

Avril wished she could have been there for him. "I'm so sorry."

He went silent for a while. "Why are you here, Avril, really?"

She gulped. It wasn't just a question. It was an order, and she had to tell him. "I think you know why," she mumbled.

Hunter's expression tensed as he nodded. "MedAct talked you into becoming my new bound one, didn't they?"

She winced. "No! I volunteered."

CHAPTER 3

Surprise filled him as Hunter stared at the brunette in front of him. He didn't like the hurt he saw in her eyes. "Why would you do that?"

"Because...I care about you. I want to give you a new chance at happiness. It always hurt every time I saw you in the media. I knew you didn't have much of a choice and that if MedAct ever managed to get their hands on you they'd try to convince you into binding yourself to a woman again. I wanted to be there when that day came." The blush on her cheeks made her even more appealing.

Avril, the sweet and cute, little twelve-year-old girl was now a woman, and he couldn't stop staring at her. Hunter heard her words, but her face kept him mesmerized.

"You can't see me as your bound one, can you?"

Her question took him off guard. He opened his mouth to answer but had no idea what to say.

Could she be a potential bound one for him?

Once he bound himself to her, he'd love her just as much as he'd loved Sarah, but right now? Well, he barely knew her, and besides, he'd always considered them as friends.

Nothing more. It would have been strange otherwise.

"I'm still that twelve-year-old girl in your mind, aren't I?" she asked.

"I guess, in a way, you are." He leaned forward in his chair. "Avril, why do you want to become my bound one?"

"Because if it's not me, another woman will fill that place. Because if I don't, and you refuse to bind yourself, you'll be taken away to a place I cannot go, and we'll never see each other again. Because if I don't, you'll try to escape and go back to the Fighters, and the risk of you getting hurt again is big. I don't ever want to see you get hurt again."

Hunter watched her for a while, studying her expressions and body language. There was something she wasn't telling him. She seemed too scared, too nervous, too desperate. "What's the real reason, Avril? You wouldn't put yourself through all that just to save *me*. Binding yourself to a Fighter is like asking for trouble. We're difficult, damaged, untrustworthy. Don't you know that?"

She nodded. "I know, but you smiled at me as soon as you recognized me. You'll never hurt me."

She had a point. If another woman had walked in, it would've been a completely different story. He would've never hurt the woman, but he would've scared her into changing her mind about him. He would have shown her his worst sides, but with Avril, he just couldn't do that.

"What is the real reason, Avril?" he asked again, but this time it was a demand.

Avril swallowed and shifted on her chair. She opened her

mouth. Her lips trembled. "I...I want to help you."

"So you're doing this out of guilt? You feel that you owe me because I helped you when you were a child?"

Her chin dropped and she stared at him. "No, it's not like that."

"Then how is it like? You realize that once I'm bound to you, you'll never get rid of me, right? It will be for life. You won't be able to throw me out once you grow tired of me."

She looked down.

He'd hurt her. He immediately regretted his words, but she needed to know the truth. She needed to *see* the truth and not expect a fairy tale. He couldn't say she saw it like that, but women who wanted to bind a Fighter to them baffled him. The Fighter's problems didn't go away just because a new bond was in place. He'd feel better, but his programming would still be scarred and damaged from what had once happened.

"I'll never grow tired of you," she whispered.

Confusion grew within him, but at the same time, she was definitely hiding something.

There was another reason she was doing this.

"I'm damaged, Avril."

"I know. I've read your files."

He winced. "My files?"

She nodded. "Doctor Silva showed me your files yesterday. She wanted me to be sure before you and I met."

"Of course." He sighed. "And what did my files say?"

"That your programming is severely damaged because

of the broken bond. It makes you unstable and gives you restless nights. You switch easily between emotions and anger controls you. You know, all that could be fixed if you bound yourself to me."

Hunter snorted. "I guess she got the chance to examine me when I was asleep."

"No, I don't think so. She told me they wouldn't do that against your will."

He snorted. "Against my will? She drugged me over and over again. Where was my will then?" He glared at the one-way window. He couldn't see through it, but instincts told him Jade was on the other side of it.

If she tried something like that again, he'd make her pay. He wouldn't physically hurt her, but intimidation was something he was good at.

Yes, his anger drove him. It'd been his partner since Sarah had died, but it'd also kept him alive.

Living among the Fighters wasn't easy. Most had some sanity left. He was one of them and because of that, he was able to help Nightmare with his goals, but some Fighters had to be kept restrained. Not only were they a danger to others, but also to themselves. Fighters had attacked him for no reason on several occasions.

Some had so badly damaged programming they'd been beyond saving and their lives had been terminated with a bullet through the head. It had been fast and easy, ending their suffering.

Living with plenty of unstable cyborgs created many

unpleasant situations, but despite that, they stuck together. After all, they only had each other, and nowhere else to go. They only had each other to rely on because as soon as they stepped outside their safe walls, they were either chased by the police or MedAct's cyborg soldiers.

The police wanted to kill them. MedAct wanted to bind them to new bound ones. Neither appealed to a Fighter.

Despite the pain in their hearts, most preferred remaining unbound because the bond wasn't real. And yet, here he was, with sweet Avril in front of him, and considering belonging to her...because he was tired...

The revelation was just as shocking as Sarah's death had been, but in the end, he'd never allow it to happen. It didn't matter how sick and tired he was of being a Fighter.

Besides, Avril was doing this for the wrong reasons. He refused to be bound to someone who wanted to help him out of guilt. That had to be her reasoning, even if she said otherwise.

There was a knock on the door before it opened. A cyborg soldier came in, pushing a cart filled with food. The aroma of mashed potatoes, chicken legs, and dark gravy hit Hunter in the face. It was all put on elegant porcelain bowls. Next to the bowls were two plates, two sets of cutleries, and a container filled with vegetables.

There were also plenty of sodas, a can of water, and a can of orange juice. Since he was a cyborg, he ate a lot, but there was more than enough on the cart for two people. Apparently, Jade had expected him to eat with Avril.

Two days without eating had taken its toll on his body. Hunter was weak and his mouth watered when he saw all the deliciousness. The drug that'd been used on him had made him even weaker, but he'd tried not to show how bad he actually felt.

He didn't want anyone to know that his knees were shaking even when he was sitting, or that his hands felt like heavy bricks when he tried to lift them. He wanted them to think that he was fine.

The cyborg soldier left the room without a word.

Hunter met Avril's gaze. "Hungry?"

She seemed surprised by the question.

"You don't expect me to eat all this, do you? I know cyborgs eat a lot, but even I can't get all this down."

She blushed. "I'd love to have a piece."

"Good."

Thankfully, the chains around his wrists were long enough for him to pull the cart closer. Once it stood by the table, he grabbed the plates. Hunter put one in front of him and one in front of her. He enjoyed having her eyes on him as he set the table. It even made him grin when he spotted her gentle smile filled with anticipation.

He was thankful that she was here. Not because she wanted to become his new bound one, but because there'd been someone out there throughout the years thinking of him. It moved his heart, and the long-lost happiness slowly awakened within him again as he placed some mashed potatoes on his plate. "How much do you want?" he asked and put a big spoon of potatoes on her plate.

"I can do it myself. You don't have to—"

"But I want to. So, how much?"

Her cheeks reddened even more.

Hunter liked that color on her. She hadn't been one of the most outgoing children, but she'd never been afraid of trying new things or standing up for her opinion. He saw strength in her. He always had. Her being here was proof enough of her willingness to fight for him.

"Um...one more spoon, please."

He gave her another spoonful before he placed two chicken legs on her plate. "Gravy?"

"Yes, please."

He actually enjoyed this more than he'd anticipated. His life with Sarah had been wonderful, but he'd never been given the chance to feed her. Sarah had been a private person and she'd often needed to be on her own. It hadn't bothered him in the beginning because it had been put inside his programming. But over the years, his programming had changed.

Hunter had started to grow into a person of his own and it hadn't taken him long to realize that he needed more than Sarah had been able to give. Although, he hadn't been miserable. He'd been happy, but there'd been a feeling of dissatisfaction.

He couldn't help but wonder if it would be the same with Avril.

"There you go," he said after pouring the gravy onto her plate.

"Thank you." She spooned some vegetables on her plate.

Apparently, he wasn't allowed to do it for her. It only made him grin. Hunter filled his plate with twice as much food as hers. It took him only a few seconds. He was starving and the rumbling in his stomach told him to hurry. He grabbed his fork and started eating.

After all their talking, it felt strange when the room suddenly fell into a long silence. All that was heard were the clanking sounds of silverware on ceramic. They exchanged gazes from time to time, and he enjoyed the smile she gave him, but he didn't like the sadness in her eyes. Maybe she understood it would never work between them.

Once they were done, the silence remained.

He didn't know what to say.

"So what happens now?" Avril asked after a while.

Hunter licked his lips. He didn't want to say it, but he had to. "Go home, Avril."

She winced "What?"

"Go home."

"Why?"

"I appreciate you wanting to help me, and I'm glad you still consider me a friend, but I cannot bind myself to a woman who wants me for the wrong reasons."

She turned pale. "The wrong reasons?"

He nodded. "You want to bind me to you because of guilt, even if you don't believe so yourself. I helped you in the past and now you want to return the favor."

"But that's not—"

He raised his hand and she went silent. "You have a good heart. I know you mean well, but binding myself to you means I'll fall in love with you. That's what the bond is. Love. Even if it's not true love the emotions will feel real. The problem is ... you won't love me back. That's a relationship doomed to fail."

Avril opened her mouth to say something, but nothing came out. The color drained from her face, but Hunter couldn't stop. He had to break this up before she thought there was any hope for them.

"I'm sorry, Avril. It's for the best. I survived Sarah's death, but I won't survive a second loss. My programming is too damaged. Not even a new bond will save me from that fate."

She sat stunned as tears gathered in her eyes.

Hunter hated himself for doing this to her.

The door to the interrogation room opened and Jade came in. Two cyborg soldiers followed her.

"I'd like to be taken back to my room now," he told her. "I did what we agreed to."

"Of course."

He'd expected the doctor to protest, but she didn't.

One cyborg unlocked his chains, and he stood. His body was stronger from the food, but he wasn't well yet. The drug was still in his system, but by tomorrow, he'd be recovered.

Avril rose from her chair.

He approached her. "I'm glad I got the chance to see you again."

She still didn't say anything. The sadness in her eyes made

him think he'd awakened her from her hopeless dream, but the last thing he wanted was to hurt Avril.

Hunter and Sarah had always liked having Avril over. She'd never been an issue and he'd thought about her a few times over the years, wondering what had become of the young girl who'd always looked up to him. Now he knew, and he had to let her go again.

He reached toward her face without a second thought, but when he realized what he was doing, he immediately pulled back. The pain in Avril's eyes grew and he cursed on the inside, but he couldn't risk touching her.

"I'm sorry. I can't touch you. Have a nice life, Avril."

Without another word, he grabbed the rose, a memory of her he'd cherish as long as it blossomed.

He headed for the door. The two cyborg soldiers followed right behind him.

CHAPTER 4

Avril watched Hunter go. She hadn't expected it to hurt this much. He'd said goodbye. He didn't want anything to do with her and that ate her up from the inside.

"I thought it be for the best to interrupt when he told you to go home. It was obvious he'd made up his mind," Jade said.

She tried to pull herself together, but her emotions lived like a wildfire within her. "He doesn't want anything to do with me."

"That's because he believes you're here for the wrong reasons."

Avril shook her head. "I'm not."

"Tell him how you feel."

"He wouldn't let me."

"Hunter is a stubborn cyborg. Let him cool down for the rest of the day and try again tomorrow. I can bring him here again."

"No, not here. Let me go to his room where we'll have privacy," Avril said.

The doctor raised an eyebrow. "That can be dangerous.

There are no cameras in his room, and if he snaps, you'll be dead before we're able to reach you."

Avril swallowed nervously. She hadn't experienced Hunter unstable today, but it didn't mean he wasn't. One shared meal wasn't enough to know how he really felt. Neither was a smile or two. But she had to know. "I'm willing to take the risk. If you want me to sign anything to prove I'm serious, then I will."

Jade studied her. "I understand, and no, you don't need to sign anything. You did that your first day here."

Avril nodded. She'd signed tons of papers the first day at MedAct's school. There hadn't been much to learn about the Fighters, though, but the teachers had stated many times they were dangerous and unstable.

During the course, many women had been told to leave because they hadn't taken it seriously. They'd believed becoming the bound one of a Fighter would be an exciting adventure, and that wasn't acceptable. Only a few had been allowed to finish the course. The last thing she wanted now was to fail. Hunter meant too much to her.

"To be on the safe side, I'll place a cyborg soldier outside Hunter's room, and that's not up for debate."

Avril winced. "But what if he and I—"

The doctor's lips twitched. "A bonding can be wild, and you don't want the cyborg to rush in just because you scream, am I right?"

She could only nod.

"How about a safe word?"

Avril liked that idea. "Like what?"

"How about *'help*?"

She couldn't help but laugh. Jade's attempt to ease her mood worked. "Yeah, they can't mistake that one."

Just because things hadn't gone so well today, it didn't mean they wouldn't go better next time. The doctor had told her she had as much time as she needed to make Hunter come around. The only way he'd ever be safe again was with her. As a Fighter, he'd always be hunted, either by the police or by MedAct. "Hunter said that love within a bond isn't real. What did he mean by that?"

"The Fighters believe the bond isn't real, that they can live without it, but that's not true. If they lose their bound one, most of them will die. It was how they were created because there was no other way. They just refuse to see that, and that's also why they choose to stay unbound. But that's also why their bonds scream inside of them. Their programming is desperate for a bond so an intimate touch will be enough to bind them again if an unbound woman touches them. At least, we think so."

Avril clenched her fists. "Hunter wanted to touch me, but he pulled back."

She nodded. "That proves our suspicions might be true, but we need to know more to be sure."

"I will try to find out more about it tomorrow."

Jade smiled. "Thank you. Go and rest now. Tomorrow will be a long day."

CHAPTER 5

Avril was a wreck when she approached the room where Hunter was being held the following morning. She was at one of MedAct's top floors. The hallway was wide and bright with doors on both sides.

She'd barely slept. The chaos in her head had kept her awake. She was even more nervous today than she'd been yesterday. This time, Hunter knew why she was here, and he'd fight her.

The question was, if she failed today too, should she keep trying or let Hunter go? Jade had told her she had all the time in the world, but if she kept trying, would Hunter start despising her?

The doctor waited by the door, but she wasn't alone. A handsome cyborg soldier with blond hair was there too. He reminded Avril of a mountain with his tall frame and muscular body. His shoulders were as wide as two of her and he could probably touch the ceiling if he reached for it.

He gave her a short nod as she came closer. He had those typical shining cyborg eyes, and to her surprise, there was kindness in them even if the rest of his expression was stern.

She'd never been fond of the cyborg soldiers. They all reminded her more of machines than human beings and they seemed to do nothing but follow orders.

They were all bound, but she'd never seen any of the people they belonged to. She found that weird since cyborgs didn't want to be too far away from their bound one.

"Good morning." Jade smiled.

"Good morning," Avril answered.

"This is Soul," Jade said. "He'll guard you while you're with Hunter. If anything goes wrong, just call for help and he'll be by your side within seconds."

She swallowed and nodded, didn't doubt that Soul was a trained soldier. His black clothing, straight posture, and the gun by his hip made her wonder what it was like to be bound to one of his kind. The cyborg soldiers hadn't been mentioned during her course. She knew even less about them than about the Fighters.

"Are you ready?" Jade asked.

Avril looked at the door that led to Hunter's room and nodded. She wasn't ready, but she had to do this.

The doctor used a key-disk. She pressed it against a metallic plate. There was a click and the door opened.

The first thing Avril noticed was a short hallway and how dark it was. Why weren't the lights on? Worry awakened within her as she exchanged gazes with Jade. She seemed worried, too.

"Soul," the doctor said.

"I'm on it," the cyborg soldier said and pulled out his

rifle. He walked inside with slow and wary steps while they waited.

Avril's heart pounded. The waiting felt like an eternity as she listened to Soul moving around inside the room. She'd no idea what it looked like in there, but she had a bad feeling that something was wrong...very wrong.

"You may come in," he finally called, and Avril hurried inside.

Jade followed her.

She came to a halt after walking past the small hallway. The room was about two hundred square feet, with a simple bed placed in a corner and a small wardrobe by the other corner. There was another door inside the room. She assumed it led to the bathroom.

Two small windows were placed by the ceiling. They were barely big enough to fit an arm through, probably to keep the Fighters from escaping.

Soul stood in the middle of the room, looking at Hunter, who sat curled up on the bed. He glared at them with his shining eyes, and Avril's heart broke when she saw his state.

His hair was a tangled mess and his shirt looked like a torn rag that would fall off any second. Blood was smeared on his face and it seemed to be coming from his bloodied knuckles. There were holes in the walls all over the room with traces of blood.

"Oh, my God," Avril gasped. She took a step toward him, but Soul grabbed her arm and shook his head.

"Don't go near him. He's not stable," the cyborg said.

"But—"

"Soul's right," Jade said. "He's hurt himself and don't think for a second he won't hurt you when he's like this."

She couldn't believe this was happening. "Didn't you hear anything going on in here? He must have made a lot of noises." She gave them an accusatory glance.

"We have cyborg guards walking by here every fifteen minutes throughout the whole day, but they never heard anything. Otherwise, they would have reported it. As you know, cyborgs have much better hearing than we humans do. Hunter must have heard them coming and stopped hitting the walls as they passed by."

Avril looked at Hunter again. Her emotions were tearing her apart. She wanted so badly to help him, but she had no idea what to do. Although now she knew how wrong she'd been about him.

He'd seemed stable yesterday, but this proved that his programming was more messed up than she'd believed. Even so, her determination didn't flicker. Somehow, she had to make him well again, didn't matter what it took.

"Leave," she told Soul and Jade.

They shot her a surprised look.

"Are you crazy?" Jade said. "I'm not leaving you in here alone with him. You should leave and come back when he feels better. Right now, there's nothing you can do."

"I've signed the papers," Avril said. "I know what I am doing. You need to leave. Please."

"No way."

She took a deep breath. She was ready to fight for what she believed in, and right now, that was Hunter. "I don't care what you think or want. I'm here to help Hunter and he needs me. Please, just do as I ask. I need to do this."

Avril didn't miss the anger in Jade's eyes. For a long minute, she remained silent, before she finally spoke: "Soul stays outside the room and you will not lock the door."

Avril nodded. She could agree to that. She turned her focus back to Hunter as Jade and Soul left the room.

The door closed behind them, leaving her on her own with an unstable Fighter who could kill her if she wasn't careful.

Honestly, Avril had no idea if she was doing the right thing or not, but deep down, she hoped she was.

"You should've listened to Jade," Hunter said, making her flinch from the coldness in his voice.

She clenched her fists and tried to stay strong, but it was almost impossible to do as the nerves swept over her. "I will *not* give up on you."

"I could hurt you without meaning to, Avril. I'm burning up. It literally feels like my body is on fire. Like I'm going to explode, and all I can do is scream as I'm forced to live through the havoc."

Confusion filled her. "Why does it feel like that?"

"Because of you! It's all *your* fault."

Avril held her breath. A frigid chill traveled through her spine, and for a split second, she considered leaving. There was nothing but pure anger in his shining eyes, and that rage was directed at her. "I don't understand. What have I done?"

"My bond wants me to accept you as my bound one. It has never reacted this strongly to a woman before, but for some reason, you're driving it crazy. I'm trying to hold it back, but the more I fight, the more I lose."

She licked her lips. "Would it be so bad being bound to me, Hunter?"

"Yes! I believe my bond has chosen you because of our friendship in the past, but you can't base a relationship on that. Once I'm bound to you, I'll crave you in ways you can't even grasp yet."

She dared to take one step closer to him, but it only made him tense.

"Stay away. I don't want you, doesn't matter what my bond tells me. I won't be happy with you."

Her heart slid to her stomach and agony washed over her. She tried to hide the pain, but it wasn't easy. Tears burned her eyes. "On the contrary. I believe you'd be very happy with me."

His gaze darkened. There was a flicker in his eyes that didn't seem to stop. The shining increased and then decreased, over and over again. She had no idea what it meant but assumed his bond was the cause.

The way he threw his head around wasn't promising. It was almost as if he hung on a thin thread that would break any second. And when that second came, he'd attack her.

Avril had to be careful. He was many times stronger and

bigger in every possible way.

He could break her into two without even breaking a sweat.

She took another step toward him, even if she was playing with fire.

Hunter pressed himself against the wall and showed his teeth. "I'm warning you, Avril. Stay away. I will not bind myself to you."

"Why? Do you find me unattractive? Are you repulsed by me?"

He winced. "Of course not. Why would you think that? You've no idea how much I want to touch you, and that's why you're dangerous to me. I didn't recognize you at first, but once I did, all I wanted was to hold you. I remembered how protective I was of you when you were a child, and my bond remembered it, too. Now, it wants to protect you as my bound one."

Joy filled her, pushing away some of that wariness she felt toward him. "You feel overprotective of me?"

"Yes, damn it!" he hissed. "But this time, it's not like when you were a child. This time, my bond sees you as an adult woman. It screams inside my head like crazy, telling me to rip your clothes off and to take you hard against the wall."

Heat rushed her body as she couldn't help but imagine what he'd just said. "Then why don't you?"

The shining in his eyes intensified as his anger grew. "Because you want to bind me to you for the wrong reasons!"

She shook her head and tried to remain calm as he got louder. "No, I don't."

Hunter flew up from the bed, but he didn't approach her. "Yes, you do! Don't lie to me!"

Avril took a deep breath. It was time to tell him. "I'm doing this because I love you."

CHAPTER 6

Shock went through Hunter like a wave of cold air. His bond reacted by going just a little bit crazier. It made him groan when the need to go to her intensified. His heartbeat increased and he was unable to pull his gaze from hers.

She just stood there, several feet away, staring. Her eyes were sad, but her posture was relaxed.

Damn, she was so beautiful...and he wanted her badly...

"You love me?"

Avril nodded. "Yes, I always have."

With those simple words, she gave his bond the last piece it needed to initiate. All he had to do now was to touch her and his eyes would flash. Hunter felt a strong and uncontrollable pull toward her, and as in a trance, he took one step closer. He reached out, unable to stop listening to the mantra that played inside his head.

Touch her. Bond with her. Touch her. Bond with her...

He was losing the battle. He wasn't going to be able to resist much longer.

For twenty years, he'd fought against the bond, trying to keep it in check. Losing Sarah had devastated him, but somehow, he'd managed to keep himself in control. When it came to Avril, that control was gone. The bond saw her as the perfect candidate.

She lifted her palm toward him and took a step back. "Stop, Hunter."

He jerked to a halt. "Fuck." Hunter backed away.

That had been close. One more step and he would've touched her. It didn't even need to be an intimate touch anymore. His bond was so worked up it wasn't funny.

Hunter sat on the bed, resignation filling him. His hands hurt, especially his knuckles from hitting the walls, but he ignored the pain. "Why did you stop me?" he asked. "I thought you wanted me to bind myself to you."

"I do, but not like this. I want it to be on your terms. Not on mine or your bond's."

He relaxed and smiled. "Thank you, Avril. That means the world to me."

"Do you want me to leave?" she asked.

Hunter took a deep breath. "It'd calm my need to bond with you if you did, but no, I want you to stay. I want you to tell me more about your feelings for me. You said you've loved me a long time. Did you love me when you were a child, too?"

Avril nodded. "Back then, it was more of a childish crush. You and Sarah were my whole world, but I often wished I'd meet someone like you one day."

"So, you're here because you love me." Hunter had to say it aloud to actually believe it. It sounded almost too good to be true, but he didn't doubt her words. He had no idea why he trusted her on this, when he'd called her a liar just a few minutes ago. Maybe it was because it made him happy to hear it.

"Yes," she said. "I hope that's the right reason."

His lips twitched. It sure was. "I never knew."

"You were bound to Sarah and you wouldn't have taken a twelve-year-old girl's crush seriously."

Hunter agreed. "Tell me, Avril. What would life be like with you?"

She licked her lips. "I hope it will be a happy one. I am determined to make it work. I don't have much to offer, but I'm sure we can create the life we want ... together." She reached toward him.

"You want to hold me?" he asked.

"Yes. You have no idea how much."

He stood up and looked straight at her, but didn't move closer. It made her lower her hands. "It won't be easy, Avril, even if the bond is in place. I have so many issues because of my damaged program. Are you really ready for that?"

"Yes. I want to stand by your side, and help you through it all. I've never abandoned you, and I never will. I'm here because I love you, and because I'd do anything to see you well again."

There was seriousness in her eyes, and his trust for her grew stronger.

Hunter became more and more certain that Avril knew what she was doing and that she didn't believe in a fairy tale between them.

It was funny, but he was actually considering binding himself to her.

Yesterday, he'd been sure it'd never happen. Today, he yearned for her. He wanted to rest in her arms. Wanted to close his eyes, lean his head against her chest, and just listen to the sounds of her heartbeat. He'd find more healing there, in her embrace, than anywhere else. It'd bring him calmness, it'd bring him peace.

So why was he still hesitating?

Hunter had no idea how to answer to the things she'd just said, so he just nodded. Too many emotions lived inside him. He wanted to grab her hand and initiate the bonding process, but at the same time, he wanted to stand here, away from her.

After all, he had a duty to the Fighters. Nightmare needed him. Not many of the Fighters were suitable for the things Nightmare needed help with. He was one of them, and he had information that could be fatal for the Fighters.

But he was so tired....just so damn tired...

Twenty years had passed since Sara's death. He'd been with the Fighters most of that time. He'd seen a lot. Experienced a lot. He'd become close to many of them, and he'd helped many of the new ones to adapt, just like Nightmare had helped him.

However, the thing Hunter remembered most was the pain and suffering, mostly emotional suffering caused by the broken bond. Avril could take all that away. She could give him a chance for a good life again. It wouldn't be easy, but things would get better in time.

No more fighting, no more robbing places for sustenance. No more killing, or having to watch other Fighters lose it. No more having to watch them being terminated.

Avril loved him.

That alone brought him some calmness while the thought of returning to the Fighters filled him with stress.

He took a step closer to her.

She tensed and insecurity filled her eyes.

It was an insecurity he felt himself. It was as if two sides of him struggled. He wasn't sure yet, but considering his options, she was the best one.

Getting him out would be difficult for Nightmare. With Silver, it'd been planned. With him, nothing was planned. He hadn't been able to escape after Nightmare, Edge, Heaven, and himself had been brought out of the house to be taken to MedAct.

Nightmare had tried to remove Shade's bond to Phoebe. Hunter hadn't liked it but had agreed to go through with it for the greater good. Unfortunately, it hadn't worked. He had no idea if Shade was still alive, but he'd seen the cyborg struggle and he'd seen how it'd affected him. It hadn't gone in the right direction.

"Hunter," he heard Avril say, bringing him back to the present.

He met her gaze and gave her a gentle smile. He was calm now. Didn't feel like hitting the wall again, but there was a gaping, emotional hole inside his chest, and it only grew bigger.

"You don't have to decide now," she said. "We have all the time in the world."

"And what if I, in the end, tell you no? Will you be able to let me go?"

She clenched her fists. She was fighting with herself. That told him how much she really wanted him. There was desire in her eyes, and the need to go to him radiated through her whole being. "Yes, I'll let you go if that is what you decide." Her words didn't come easy, but Avril was ready to sacrifice her happiness for his. She wouldn't force him into a bond, and that made him want her even more.

It wasn't a mystery, what awaited if he told her no. If he didn't manage to escape, MedAct would transfer him somewhere.

They said it was a place where cyborgs like him could live in peace, but he wouldn't have any communication with the outside world. All Fighters feared that place. They doubted it even existed. It sounded more like they'd be taken to their execution because there was no information to be found about that place. It didn't even have a name.

"But you don't want to let me go, do you?"

"No, never." Her voice was almost a whisper.

There was a knock on the door, and Hunter's anger flared.

Whoever had knocked didn't wait. Instead, the door opened, and a second later, Doctor Silva entered.

To his surprise, she seemed angry, too. No, she looked *furious*. Considering how unstable he was right now, that was the last emotion she should show in front of him if she wanted him to co-operate.

He tensed and prepared for a fight.

Jade stopped in front of Avril and looked her in the eyes before she looked at him. "We have a situation."

CHAPTER 7

Avril didn't like the seriousness in Jade's voice. "What kind of situation?"

The doctor held a tablet in her hands. Hunter slowly came closer with narrowed eyes. His suspicion was impossible to miss.

"We've received a video from Nightmare, and I need you two to watch it." She switched the tablet on. "He demanded we get back to him within an hour after viewing it."

There probably wasn't anyone out there who didn't know who Nightmare was. Avril had seen him several times in media. He was a dark, handsome cyborg with a scar on his throat that everyone feared. He was the Fighters' leader, and he was also the most intimidating cyborg she'd ever seen. Hopefully, she'd never need to come face-to-face with him.

The doctor pushed a few digital buttons on the screen and a holographic image rose. The video started to play.

At first, Avril wasn't sure what she was looking at, but it was showing the inside of a big room. On the floor sat five small children pressed together with two women, who wore terrified expressions. They hugged the children to them, and some were crying. Something told her nothing good could come out of this.

The camera moved around in the room, taking in the children and the adults while spotting Fighters dressed in black, with huge rifles in their hands, rifles that were pointed at the hostages.

And then Nightmare came into view.

Avril gasped. Even if he wasn't in the same room as she, he was still intimidating. She'd never seen so much anger and determination in someone's eyes before.

For a short moment, he just stared into the camera. It sent cold chills down her spine.

She expected to see anticipation or some kind of positive feeling in Hunter's features from seeing Nightmare, but she didn't. To her surprise, she saw sadness.

"I doubt I need any introduction," Nightmare said, "and I think you also know why I'm contacting you. You're holding one of my men in custody, and I want him back. I'm sure you know who I'm talking about." He took a step away from the camera and pointed at the children and two adults. "I hate doing this, but you give me no choice. You either release Hunter within the hour from when you see this video, or I'll silence them all for good." The leader looked into the camera again, standing closer than before. Fury shone in his eyes. "Do I make myself clear? I'm waiting for your reply."

A phone number showed up in the video for a few seconds before the holographic image disappeared.

Silence filled the room and all Avril heard were her own hectic breaths. "Oh, my God," she gasped.

Jade sighed and lowered the tablet. "I honestly never believed he'd sink this low. He's done a lot of crazy and stupid things in the past, but he's never hurt children before. Either he's bluffing, or something has snapped in his head."

"He wants me back," Hunter said.

Those words seared like hell in Avril's heart. All her hope for a future with Hunter went out the window. It'd all been in vain. Hunter would never be hers. He would never choose her now.

"He does," Jade said, "but I'm surprised by how far he's willing to go to get you back. You must be special to him."

Hunter didn't answer.

"We've had plenty of Fighters in our custody that Nightmare didn't even raise a finger to get back. So why is he ready to kill innocent children to get *you* back?"

He remained silent.

"Time is running out, Hunter. It's been twenty minutes since the other doctors and I watched this video for the first time. We've barely forty minutes to call him back."

Hunter finally sighed. "If you want that information, you'll have to drill it out of me."

Frustration flashed in her eyes. "You know, sometimes I really hate the rule that forbids me to do things to you."

Hunter's gaze narrowed. "So you're no better than Nightmare."

Jade raised a warning finger. "Don't ever compare me

to him. Just because I say that rule pisses me off, it doesn't mean I don't think it is a good rule."

He snorted. "Whatever."

Avril's chin trembled. "What do you intend to do?"

She took a deep breath. "I don't think there's much we can do. Maybe Nightmare is faking it, but at the same time, maybe he isn't. If he wants Hunter back, then I'll give him Hunter. I'm not going to let innocent children die just because I want to keep a Fighter. I'm not going to risk it. I hope you understand, Avril."

Her heart broke into a thousand pieces. Tears burned her eyes. Now it wasn't just her chin that trembled. Her whole body shook. Her knees were weak. Her head spun and a headache wasn't far away.

She wanted to scream, she wanted to let the world know how much it hurt to lose him again, but she remained still as she dried her tears away. Avril nodded and sobbed. "I understand." She didn't want to look up at Hunter, but couldn't stop herself. There was sympathy in his eyes. She wished she hadn't seen it. That was the last thing she wanted from him.

It only made her feel worse.

"I'll call him and put an end to this," Jade said before she turned to Hunter. "You'll be free soon. You must be thrilled." She spoke her words without a single sign of amusement.

Hunter didn't answer.

Avril had no idea what went on inside his mind. He just stood still and watched; his gaze went slowly between them before he clenched his fists and looked down. He didn't seem happy with the news that he'd be released soon. She couldn't help but wonder why. Maybe he hadn't expected it.

Avril saw her happiness fade away with each digital button Jade pressed as she entered the phone number Nightmare had left in the video.

For a short while, there was nothing but the dial signal.

On the fourth one, Nightmare answered and a holographic image of his face rose from the tablet. His eyes were cold, his expression filled with anger, and when his gaze set on Jade, his rage seemed to grow.

"Well, you took your time to pick up," Jade snorted. "I was starting to think you didn't miss Hunter that much after all."

"And you sure called fast," Nightmare retorted. "You must want me bad."

The doctor's gaze darkened. "Yeah, tied down and locked away."

Nightmare gave her an evil grin. "I didn't know you had such wicked dreams about me, Jade. Keep dreaming, and who knows, maybe one day, they'll come true."

Jade looked taken aback for a second. "If you want to keep your body parts where they are, you better make sure that never comes true."

Avril blinked. She couldn't believe her own ears. They went on like an old couple. The doctor didn't seem afraid to insult Nightmare and it was obvious they knew each other, but to Avril, he was as frightening as the unknown things that lurked in the night.

Nightmare ignored Jade and looked at Hunter. "Are you all right?"

Hunter nodded. "I'm fine. They haven't hurt me."

"Good. They would've regretted it if they had."

Then his gaze turned to her and Avril froze in place. It felt like he splashed her with ice cold water with his cold look.

"Who are you?" he asked.

His question made her jump, but she tried not to show how he affected her. "I'm...um...Avril."

He narrowed his eyes and gave her a once-over. "I haven't seen you before. Are you a new doctor?"

She shook her head. "No, I'm not a..." She didn't finish her sentence because he flashed his teeth. Instinctively, she took a step back and gasped.

"You're trying to bind Hunter to yourself, aren't you?"

"I..." Avril wanted to say the final decision was Hunter's, but the words didn't come.

Hunter took a step closer. "Don't scare her, Nightmare. Avril is a friend from when I was bound to Sarah. She means well."

"I don't care. You know the bond isn't real, and the last thing you want is to end up trapped with a new one."

"You've nothing to worry about. They're letting me go."

Surprise filled Nightmare's eyes. "Just like that?" He snorted. "Maybe I should try this method with every Fighter that gets caught." He gave Jade a wicked grin that promised trouble.

275

It made Jade sigh.

"I'll let him go as soon as you guarantee the children and the women are safe," she said.

Nightmare remained silent for a while, just studying the doctor. "Fine. We'll leave as soon as our small talk is over. I'll text you the address where the children and the women are so you can send a group of cyborg soldiers to check up on them."

Jade nodded. "Agreed."

Hunter took a deep breath and wrinkled his forehead as he raised his hand. He wore a pained expression that worried Avril. He didn't seem all right, even if he'd said he was.

"Nightmare...wait..." Hunter said.

"Yes?"

"I..." He took another deep breath, as if he was preparing himself. "I want to stay."

Everyone in the room jumped from surprise.

Avril's jaw dropped and she watched Hunter as joy and disbelief filled her. Did he really mean it?

Nightmare stared at Hunter with shock written all over his face. "Have you lost your mind?"

"Please understand. I'm tired."

"You can rest when you get back."

He shook his head. "I don't mean that kind of tired. I'm fed up with it all to the point that it makes me sick. I'm tired of the pain and the nightmares. I'm tired of the sadness and the loneliness. I've no idea how you do it, but these twenty years are enough for me. I can't take it anymore."

If Nightmare's eyes could have caught fire, they'd be burning. "The bond isn't real."

"I know. Believe me, I know, but I still choose it, because I also know that once I return, you're going to have to put a bullet through my head in the near future. I'm losing it. I feel it. I'm hanging on a thin thread, and you know what happens when that thread snaps."

Silence filled the room.

Despite Nightmare looking like he'd explode any second, Avril felt her hope return. Hunter gave her a gentle smile and she couldn't help but smile back.

To her greatest surprise, he'd chosen her.

Nightmare finally nodded and inhaled deeply. "I understand." He turned to Jade. "He's all yours. We'll leave now and I'll send you that text." He looked at Hunter again. "Good luck, Hunter. You know what you have to do."

Hunter nodded and the line went dead.

"What did he mean by that? What is it that you have to do?" Jade asked.

"This," Hunter answered, and his gaze slowly glazed over. His arms went slack by his sides and he slumped.

Avril looked at him with confusion. "What's happening?"

Jade stood perplexed at first, but then her eyes widened, and she gasped. "Oh, crap. He is deleting information." She snatched something from her pocket.

It was a small device, no bigger than her palm. It reminded Avril of the tablet they'd watched the video on, but she doubted it was a regular tablet. It probably was a medical device of some sort. Jade started frantically pushing on digital buttons, but it was too late.

Hunter's eyes returned to normal and he gave the doctor a wry smile. "It's done. All the information about the Fighters I've gathered over the years is gone. You won't be able to get it out of me with that thing. I don't even recall where they live any longer. They're safe."

Jade didn't reply. She glared at Hunter. Anger radiated from her. Finally, she snorted, put away her device, and whirled around. With a few short steps, she was out of the room.

CHAPTER 8

Avril heard the door close behind Jade, but the doctor didn't lock it. She didn't doubt Soul remained standing in the hallway, ready to storm the room if she screamed for help, but she wouldn't. She was safe with Hunter.

Blood rushed to her face when she thought about what was to come. After all, he'd chosen her, and that meant he was willing to bind himself to her.

Hunter came closer. He raised his hand, and with a feather-light touch, caressed her cheek with the back of his hand. "How weird," he said with barely a whisper. "I can finally touch you and I'm not afraid. I'm no longer afraid of belonging to you."

She swallowed. "Are you sure about this?"

"I've never been surer about anything in my whole life. I saw the pain it caused you when you realized you'd lost me. I know your love for me is real, and I understand you're not doing this out of guilt. You really do want me."

She tensed. "Nightmare said the bond isn't real."

"It's not, but believe me, once it's in place, it will feel very real to me."

She only nodded. Avril knew how the cyborgs were constructed. Their entire existence was based on the bond. Without it, they couldn't live, didn't matter how real or fake Nightmare thought it was.

Hunter took another step closer, invading her personal space. "Once I kiss you, there'll be no turning back. You'll be stuck with me until the day you die. And when that day comes, we'll die together. I will not survive another broken bond, and I'm glad I won't. The pain is too much to handle." He licked his lips. "Each bonding is different, but I'm so starved for a bond, the process will initiate with one simple kiss."

Avril couldn't stop herself from giggling. It made Hunter smile. For the first time since her childhood, he seemed happy, and she was happy with him.

He placed his hands on her arms. "Are you ready?"

She nodded and tried to control her erratic breathing. "I'm ready."

Slowly, he leaned toward her lips, stopping inches away, giving her one last look, and then...he kissed her.

Chills flittered through her entire body as she felt his soft warm lips against hers. Goosebumps awakened on Avril's skin as Hunter's arms wrapped around her, pressing her closer to his strong muscular body.

She opened to his kiss as he deepened it. A moan escaped her throat and she reached out her tongue to meet his, but he suddenly froze, not reacting to anything she was doing.

Avril took a step back and looked up at him. He was

looking her in the eyes, but his gaze was far away. It was as if he was there, but at the same time, wasn't. Was this part of the bonding process?

All she knew was what MedAct had told her; that his eyes had to flash three times before the bond would be in place.

The first flash initiated the bond, the second accepted her, and the third sealed it.

"Hunter?" She waved her hand in front of his eyes.

There was no reaction.

Then, without a warning, a short but intense flash came from his eyes, almost blinding her.

She jerked with surprise.

His eyes had flashed!

It'd worked. Avril almost couldn't believe it. Joy filled her, making her laugh. She didn't stop the tears from running down her cheeks.

Hunter blinked several times and straightened his back as he came back to her. He frowned, as if in confusion before he met her gaze. Then he grinned. "It has begun," he said.

"I saw it. I didn't expect it to be that intense."

"It'll be even more intense within a minute, my dear." He looked at her with a hunger in his shining eyes that made her shiver with anticipation. "I need to have you, and I need to have you now."

He came at her like a starved man who'd only one thing on his mind, and it made her smile. She liked seeing him going from a gentle to a wild, craving cyborg as he ripped his shirt off, revealing his well-shaped and hairless chest.

Determination was written all over his face, along with lust and desire. Avril could barely take her eyes off of him. Just the sight of his naked upper body made her warm between her legs. She'd imagined this moment so many times in so many different ways, but now, it was finally upon her, and she was sure it'd be better than she'd ever dared to imagine.

She reached to touch him, to finally feel his skin against her hand, but Hunter grabbed her hand and pulled her into his embrace.

He kissed her again. This time, the kiss was demanding and without the trace of the gentleness he'd shown her just seconds ago, but he didn't hurt her and his short beard didn't bother her. The dark and masculine groan he let out as her tongue met his made her knees weak.

Hunter started ripping off her clothes. "I'm burning up. It feels like I'm going to explode. I'm that desperate for you." He threw her shirt on the floor and went for her bra, squeezing her breasts in the process, making her shiver with pleasure as his fingertips grazed her nipples. "Can you take me without much foreplay? I promise I'll make it up to you forever after, if you just let me take you as soon as possible now."

Avril grinned as she unbuttoned her pants. "I'm more than ready for you."

The relief that filled his eyes almost made her laugh. He looked so sweet in his need.

"Thank God." Hunter threw off the rest of his clothes. He barely gave her a chance to look him over before he helped her panties off. Then he led her to the bed. He made her sit on the edge. "Lay down."

She obeyed without a doubt and parted her legs to let him come to her.

He went down on his knees and moved into position.

Avril jerked from his unexpected touch when he placed his hand against her sex. She closed her eyes and moaned as his fingers, gently but urgently examined her. Her body jolted when he pressed one finger to her most sensitive spot, making her part her legs even more, begging him to get on with it. Then Hunter shifted, and she squeaked when he pressed two fingers into her. He leaned over her and sucked one nipple into his mouth as he worked her with his fingers.

It sent her straight to heaven. It felt so damn good to have him this way. "I thought you'd—" she breathed out between two moans.

"I'm big. I need to make sure you can take me." Hunter pulled out his fingers and straightened his back. His words had made her curious.

She wanted to know what he looked like, but most of him was hidden from her sight.

His eyes widened, and he opened his mouth as her fingers wrapped around him, slowly exploring him. He hadn't been lying. He was thicker and bigger than she'd expected. It didn't scare her. Instead, she couldn't help but imagine all the fun they'd have together.

Hunter cursed. "Damn it, Avril. I'll come apart if you keep doing that."

She grinned. "Sorry."

He snorted. "You're barely sorry."

She gave him a wry smile. "No, but I'll keep doing this unless you take me."

A shudder went through him before he moved her hand away.

Avril placed her arms above her head.

Hunter moved even closer and wrapped her legs around his waist. He guided himself into her warm channel and she watched his eyes flash a second time as he entered her.

He'd accepted her.

All kinds of emotions filled her.

He was hers now.

The only thing remaining was to seal the bond, and she promised herself she'd give him everything he'd never had with Sarah. She'd make him forget all the years of pain and suffering. She'd make him the happiest cyborg alive.

His expression was pained. "Damn, you're tight."

Avril could only smile as she enjoyed having him inside her. It was the most wonderful feeling in the world, a feeling she'd imagined and fantasized about so many times. She felt so filled by him, for a short moment it hurt, but it was a good pain, and he allowed her to adapt to him before he started thrusting.

She closed her eyes as he placed his head against her chest. His arms were tightly wrapped around her hips, keeping her bottom lifted from the bed, making it easier for him to plunge.

It didn't take long for Hunter to lose control. She felt his intensity in every thrust, and she heard it in his every groan. He became almost aggressive and wild.

The air became filled with the sounds of their lovemaking, and Avril didn't doubt that Soul heard everything. Usually, that would've been embarrassing, but in this moment of passion, she didn't care.

She was with the man she loved, and he was binding himself to her. He was falling in love with her with each thrust that bound him deeper.

She opened her eyes when he lifted his head from her chest. He supported his upper body by placing his hands by placing them on either side of her. That change made him drive forward from a new angle, and it was what she needed. She tightened around him as the climax took over. Her body lurched and her toes curled as she came, unable to stop herself from screaming out how good he made her feel.

Hunter followed just seconds later. He filled her with his release as his calls mingled with hers.

She enjoyed every moment of having him this close, and there was no other place in the entire world she'd rather be.

He exhaled heavily as he collapsed on top of her, and for long minutes, all that was heard was their heavy breathing.

Avril let her hands caress his back, slowly exploring him.

"Thank you, Avril," Hunter mumbled against her skin.

"For what?"

"For everything. I haven't felt this good in a long time."

He raised his head and looked her deep in the eyes.

She watched them flash a third time, but the flash wasn't as intense as it'd been the first and second time. This time, it was just as gentle as the look in his eyes.

There was also something new in his eyes.

Love.

It was as clear as the sun on a shiny day.

"The bond is set," he said and caressed her cheek. "I'm bound to you. Now and forever."

His words made her heart jump, both from joy and anticipation but also from nervousness and insecurity. Avril finally had everything she'd ever wanted, but the future was unknown.

Would Hunter be safe now that he wasn't one of the Fighters anymore? Would Nightmare change his mind and try to get Hunter back?

They curled up in each other's arms on the bed and he put the quilt over them. "You look worried."

"I'm thinking about the future."

"Everything will be all right. I promise."

Avril frowned. "How can you be sure?"

"Knowing Jade, she'll make sure we stay here until I'm up on my feet. She won't let me out into the world before I'm stable. And honestly, I wouldn't be surprised if she makes sure we get somewhere to live behind Glaswell's walls. She's done that for other Fighters who've bound themselves again."

She blinked. "Are you sure?"

He gave her an assuring smile. "I am."

Avril relaxed. "Good." She placed her hand against his warm and muscled chest. "Thank you."

He chuckled as he pulled her closer to him. "For what?"

"For wanting me."

"I didn't need the bond to want you, Avril. You walking back into my life was enough to make me desire you."

A warm feeling spread in her body, making her smile. "I love you."

Hunter looked her deep into the eyes. "I love you too... with all my heart and soul."

THANK YOU

Thank you for reading my story. I hope you enjoyed it.
If you want more, you can now read book two,
Loved Cyborg, Celise's and Wind's story.

ABOUT THE AUTHOR

Nellie C. Lind lives in Sweden with her son, but she was born in Poland. Writing has always been one of her greatest interests. Today, she runs the publishing house, Sense of Romance.

She writes passionate paranormal romance, fantasy, and science fiction books for adult readers. You'll find all sorts of beings in her stories, such as angels, vampires, gods, and elves.

You'll also find everything from short stories to novels among her books. Keep an eye open for upcoming releases!

Website: nellieclind.com
Blog: sense-of-romance.com